Other novels available in the Jonathan Roper series

Going Underground

I Can See You

The Long Reach

Just Kill Them

ISBN: 9798632282604

Imprint: Mike Leese Communications

The Golden Shot

Michael Leese

Michael Leese is a national newspaper journalist who worked in Fleet Street for over 25 years, including 17 years at The London Evening Standard. He had always wanted to write a book, especially a crime or science fiction novel. with work, family life, and lots of other excuses, he never seemed to get around to it. Then in 2007 Michael went free-lance and finally had time to sit down and write. Born in Birmingham, his family moved to London where he spent his formative years: he and his wife now live in Dorset close to their adult autistic son.

Dedicated to all those who have been touched by the Covid-19 pandemic.

Prologue

The space was cold, dark and frightening. A blackness from which your imagination conjured terrifying sights and sounds, this was a place to be on your guard, for real monsters lived here.

Had you been unwise enough to venture inside, you would have paused to try and make sense of your surroundings. You would have heard a low-key cacophony of rustling, intermingled with sounds that you couldn't quite place. With a sudden chill, you would have realised that you weren't alone. That there were people here, waiting in the inky blackness.

What they were waiting for would soon become apparent.

As the background resonance became louder, lights powered up, revealing a cavernous auditorium and a seated audience of more than a hundred people. Every pair of eyes in the room were focused on the centre of a stage where a hooded figure, a woman, was tied securely to a post. Even from a distance, the way the victim's head slumped forward told of despair.

All around the auditorium, the gathered faces held their breath, pitching forward with a keen interest, their shoulders tightened, their tongues licked at suddenly dry lips. There could be no doubt – this was the moment they had been waiting for.

More spotlights powered up, revealing two new figures, both clearly men. Standing on the edge of the stage, they remained strangely still, as if the blossoming lights had disturbed some private conversation.

Any idea that these two were equals was quickly dispelled as the larger of the pair suddenly smashed a big hand straight into the ribs of the smaller man. The victim howled, only staying on his feet because the aggressor had grabbed hold of him.

Eventually, he settled, gingerly touching the spot where he had been hit. Breathing heavily through his mouth, he shuddered as he pressed his hands together in silent prayer – but the big man was already on him, shaking him roughly and shouting.

"This is your last chance! No more warnings!"

His victim stared at him, fearfully.

"OK. OK, let me catch my breath."

"NOW!"

The order was bellowed so loudly that the smaller man jumped – but at least it had the desired effect. He began talking into a large microphone that the aggressor had thrust into his face.

Left a bit, left a bit. Down a bit... That's a little too far. Stop, there… Sorry. I've made a mistake and gone too far… go back to the right a tiny bit, just a little bit more, very, very gently." He paused. "No, that's wrong. I meant to say go left a tiny bit, but now we need to go more left."

He was unravelling, muddling his left from his right and starting to panic. His name was William Over, a hedge fund manager aged 48 years old. Nothing in his life up to now had prepared him for this moment. He worked hard, went home to his family and gave to good causes. He was successful, ordinary and invisible; until now.

Cold sweat was running down his body as he listened to his own commands. Even he could hear the note of wheedling desperation in his voice - a long way from the commanding tone he'd been told to assume.

As he continued to speak, he focussed his eyes on the flat-screen monitor at the edge of the stage, watching the results of his directions. Every time he said left the camera jerked left, every time he said right, the camera jerked right.

He looked up. Somewhere at the back of the auditorium, the camera that relayed those instructions was attached to the sights of a powerful crossbow. The weapon was at the back of the auditorium and would be fired over the heads of the audience, adding a thrilling veneer of danger to the experience of watching. The audience had been warned repeatedly: stand up at your peril. There would be no "comfort" breaks while the show was live.

William – Billy to his friends – was attempting to align a black cross with a bullseye that was placed over the heart of the person tied to the post. His instructions were being followed by the blindfolded man who operated the weapon and would fire it on command.

British TV fans of a particular vintage would recognise that this deadly game owed rather more than a nod to a popular television series, which first aired more than fifty years ago.

All of this was, unsurprisingly, passing Billy by. What he was thinking, was how badly he needed a friend right now – and how unlikely that was to happen. His despair wasn't helped by the fact that he was still dressed in the running gear he'd been snatched in. He'd bought it in the midst of what might be described as a mid-life crisis after his wife had presented him with an ultimatum: all sex was off until he slimmed down and got fitter. He'd been tempted to say that, if it was all the same with her, he might prefer a slice of chocolate cake. Fortunately, before the words left his mouth, he'd recognised her determined expression. Deciding that trying to make a joke out of it would land him in a whole world of trouble. So he'd dutifully set out for his evening jogs, as regular as clockwork... A punctual man, he arrived home at nearly the same time each day, changed and went straight out. The routine was critical. If he gave himself any sort of thinking time, he'd be coming up with reasons to stay at home.

Which is why at 7pm, on a pleasant late spring day, he was close to Clapham Common when he was bundled off the pavement and into the back of a white Ford Transit van.

It was all over in a heartbeat, and the fading light ensured that no-one noticed anything. Even if they had seen something and reported it, what could the police do? Stop every single white van in London? It would be a near-impossible task, not one the Met would realistically consider unless it was the highest priority – and even then, it was unlikely.

So, here was Billy, in a secret studio in London, still dressed in his top of the range keep-fit gear. It had made no difference to his running skills and could do nothing to disguise how wretched he looked. His dark skin had turned grey, his face was swollen – and, to cap it off, he couldn't stop sweating. His brown eyes were darting wildly, a rat in a trap.

Until now, he had just about managed to keep a lid on his emotions; but his time had come. Any moment soon, he would have to shout, "Fire!", and the man at the back of the auditorium would pull the trigger, launching the bolt. His captors had left him in no doubt what they expected.

With his options narrowed to one, he could no longer delude himself. He broke down, sinking to his knees, crying and talking incoherently. Only after some time did the words, he spat out, between gasps for breath begin to make sense.

"I can't do this. I can't. Please don't make me."

Shrinking into himself, he covered his face with his hands as huge sobs racked his body.

Everything was captured in loving close-up by the Sony HDC 2000 Multiformat HD Camera, in black, that was filming the whole thing. Purchased in the US at $95,000, it wasn't cheap, but it was necessary if you wanted to compete on prime time. Against shows like America's Got Talent or its UK cousin, Britain's Got Talent.

Up in the gallery, the show director's eyes glittered as she studied the images. Her perfectly manicured nails tapped lightly against her desk, drumming out a discordant beat. Today was a black-themed day. Her clothes were black, her make-up black, her nails black. She even had a black headband in her dirty blonde hair and wore black jewellery. Her right arm was covered by a full sleeve of black inked tattoos. Black pins skewered her tongue, nose and eyebrows.

Licking her lips, she kept a camera glued to Billy's face as he continued to weep, his shoulders shaking. He was totally broken. The director had been hoping for this. She knew his breakdown was television gold and would be lapped up by the millions of eager viewers tuning into the show being hosted from the Dark Web.

Billy couldn't see the director, but he would have found no comfort there if he had. Down on the stage, he was too consumed by his own distress to realise what was about to happen.

But the audience did.

For such a tough-looking woman, the director had a surprisingly gentle voice, even if there was nothing gentle about what she was saying.

"I want everyone concentrating hard. There's nothing to celebrate until we get this in the bag. Now, keep it nice and steady with Camera 1."

Her instructions were noted by the operator sitting a few feet away. He nodded and refocused on his task.

Quite uncharacteristically, the director let out a low groan of pleasure. “That angle from Camera 2 is just fantastic. You can see every line on his face. I love it. Now everyone, let’s make this bigger and better...”

In the auditorium below, the audience was starting to get really excited. Billy was still weeping, so had missed that his tormentor had donned a black executioner’s hood. Camera 1 zoomed in as the executioner’s hands reached out for the sobbing man.

Billy hadn’t realised the danger until he felt the huge hands grab his throat. His terrified reaction was captured in 4k resolution. Which was so sharp that it caught the way his eyes bulged out of their sockets, while tiny blood vessels erupted in his cornea. The director groaned again, her lips forming a little moue of pleasure at what she was watching. These were the moments she lived for. She knew her work was good enough to win an Oscar; it was just that her themes were a little too adult for regular TV. She ordered the pictures to be re-run in slow motion. This would make an excellent package for the highlights reel.

“That was fantastic,” she breathed. “Now for the money shot!”

The director wasn’t given to smiling, but she seemed to be smiling now – in fact, this was the happiest that any of the crew could recall her being. Relaxing into their roles, they began to wonder if this might mean a bonus was on the cards.

The director was also thinking of money. With a bit of smart editing, she was confident that she would have a “taster” which would encourage hundreds of thousands, maybe even millions, of new punters to hand over their bitcoins for full membership. As a veteran TV man had once said, no-one ever got poor underestimating the taste of the public. And this was reality TV with extra hot sauce –

red in tooth and claw, all thanks to the power of the Dark Web.

On the stage, the hooded man let go of Billy's throat just before his victim sank into unconsciousness. Using his far superior strength, he pulled the near lifeless Billy towards the brightly lit stage where the figure was tied to a post.

Whipping her hood away, he jabbed her in the chest. "You just got lucky." The accent was hard to place, English for sure, London maybe, and something else, something nasty.

The woman, Carol Barnes, a well-known political adviser, was blonde and tiny. In her stockinged feet, she barely came up to the chest of the thug looming over her as he untied her restraints. She was trembling as he roughly pushed her towards the spot from which Billy had just been dragged.

Billy was now almost comatose, his awareness of his surroundings mercifully disintegrating. His brain conjured up an image of his wife, and he locked onto that. He offered no resistance as he was tied to the post. There were no more tears. His brain urged him to be patient. This was nearly over; then he could go home, and everything would be normal.

The man finished his work and carefully checked that Billy was secure. He didn't want him slipping at the crucial moment. It would make things untidy, and he hated untidy.

"You were told." He patted Billy's cheek, but it wasn't a kind gesture. "You had the chance, and you blew it." Then he left the stage and went back to the woman. "Are we going to have a problem?" His expression suggested he might like it if there was going to be an issue.

Carol Barnes shook her head, focused on the monitors, and started issuing instructions to the crossbow-operator stationed above. She was near collapse, but her voice remained clear as the target moved into position over the slumped man's heart. She also wanted to cry but knew there was no point. If she was going to have any chance of seeing her children again, she had to get this right.

Squinting at the monitor, she couldn't help chewing her lip. The aim was all off, and she didn't have time to waste.

"Right a bit… quite a bit… stop, stop there. Up a bit, more, more… no, too far. Just a tiny bit down. Good, good, that's almost it. Just a tiny bit to the right."

She leaned back and took a moment to check.

Perfect.

"FIRE."

The weapon was a customised crossbow with a draw weight of almost 200 pounds. It could reach a speed of 480 feet per second, so it was probably still accelerating as it arced over the audience and reached the place where Billy was standing.

The bolt would have smashed through armour. The clothes he was wearing offered no resistance at all.

The shot was perfect. It hit home with such power that, in an instant, Billy's heart was vapourised. It was so fast that he wasn't even aware of the moment he ceased to live. His body sagged, and the woman turned away, unable to look at what she had just done.

The director ordered the screen to be split. On one side, she had the woman wearing an expression of undeniable pain, mingled with relief – and, most of all, the shame that she would do exactly the same thing again if given the same choice. The second screen showed the lifeless face of the victim. The crossbow had pushed all the air out of his lungs forcing his mouth to gape open in a final indignity.

After a few moments, the screen went blank, then opened again as a man in a clown mask bounced on to the stage, like a Stephen King novel brought to life. The golden jacket he was wearing glittered as it caught the lights.

Beneath him, the audience was shouting, stamping and clapping. For a time, he let the sound roll over him. Finally, as the noise died away and the spectators, clearly in on the act, looked on in gleeful anticipation, he spoke.

"Ladies and gentlemen, wasn't that a show to die for?" It was fast becoming the most infamous catchphrase ever.

This time the applause went off the register. The audience was on their feet and clapping their hands so hard that the compere could almost feel the wind as waves of sound rolled over his head. On and on it went, until finally, it came to an end.

The clown took a deep breath.

"Ladies and gentlemen." His amplified voice was deep and strong. "Thank you for joining us today. We'll be back next week at the same time for the next episode of... The Golden Shot!"

He walked off stage and then stopped, turning around and holding his right index finger up in the air.

"Remember – it's not the taking part that counts..."

The audience shouted back the payoff, "It's the taking apart!"

1

Launceston Place is one of the many well-heeled residential streets that meander out from Kensington High Street. Part of the W8 postcode which contains some of the most expensive houses in London.

The homes finished in white stucco give off an air of tradition, solidity and affluence. Which was precisely what the architects intended when they first came up with the designs almost two centuries ago.

It's not the most expensive part of London, but you still need deep pockets to live here.

This morning, at 7am, the shiny black front door of a house close to the Kensington High Street end of the road opened. A smartly dressed man, wearing a dark blue Chester Barrie suit, white shirt and pink tie, emerged. Stopping for a moment to enjoy his surroundings - something he did every morning.

The man standing on the step was Peter Webb. An only child, he'd inherited the house from his mother after her death fifteen years ago when he was just thirty years old. He had short brown hair, and a gentle smile was never far from his face. Everyone said he was easy company.

The fact he was an accountant, a partner in a firm based in Shepherd's Bush, tended not to turn that easy company into great company. He could get fixated on facts and figures – but people tended to like him since he was polite and interested, a somewhat unusual combination in this day and age.

He also had a secret passion. At least, he thought it was a secret, as anybody who met him could testify. He loved to talk about his obsessive support for Chelsea football club and was a season ticket holder at nearby Stamford Bridge.

On Saturday he was planning on taking his son, Edward, to a home game. The boy was, like him, an only child. It seemed to be a trait for the Webb men since Peter's father, and his father before him had been only children as well. It helped explain how the house had managed to be passed, intact, through the family over many years.

In that sense, he was blessed. Careful to remind himself regularly of his good fortune, he made an effort to never do anything that might change the direction of his luck. He took rules very seriously and made sure he never broke or even bent, them.

Glancing back at the door, he smiled at the thought that his wife and son would soon be reaching for the cups of tea he had left on their respective bedsides. Edward would be out soon – he needed to be at his private school, Westminster, by 8am – but Peter himself had an early meeting with his boss, Gerald Stone, and he did not want to be late.

Happy that all was well with the world, he walked down the steps and climbed into his electric car, a metallic blue Nissan Leaf. His wife, Liz, had persuaded him to buy it two years ago. While he liked it, he had never lost his fear that, because it was so quiet, pedestrians might not hear it and step in front of the vehicle.

As he pulled away from the curb, a large white van stopped to let him out, the blinking indicator showing it wanted to take his place. Moments later, as he set off up the road, he looked in his rear-view mirror and saw the vehicle pulling into the slot he had just vacated. For just a moment, he felt a sense of resentment at the van taking his place;

then he shook it off as being silly. He tried to make out the writing on the front of the vehicle and, despite the mirror effect putting it upside down, he could make out the words 'civil engineering'. Driving further away, he noticed two similar vans already parked up.

He joined the main traffic near an entrance to Kensington Gardens that was close to Kensington Palace, home to members of the Royal Family. He never failed to recall that magical day when he'd seen Princess Diana stride past, looking impossibly glamorous as her security kept close behind. One excited delivery driver had even shouted "Alright Di?" at her and had been stunned into silence when she rewarded him with a huge smile. Bringing his thoughts back to the journey, he turned left and headed towards Shepherd's Bush.

Despite his best efforts, as he drove, his thoughts kept returning to the work vans arriving outside his home. Perhaps it meant one of his neighbours was planning some building work, and he shuddered at the potential turmoil. If it was a major project, like a basement dig out, it would last forever. As soon as he got a moment at work, he would go online. And check if there was anything he could find on the planning applications site maintained by Kensington and Chelsea council.

At about the same time as he was navigating the final leg of his journey. His son Edward – who was a younger clone of his father – emerged from the house and noticed several workmen were lurking nearby, apparently waiting for something.

Putting his head down, careful to avoid eye contact, he set off at a brisk pace.

"Like gaming, do you?"

The question brought him up short. Like most 15-year-old boys, he was obsessed with videogames and would have happily played all day, every day, if he could have got away with it.

Looking up, he saw one of the workmen smiling at him in a friendly fashion. The man waved his hand about in a vague way that seemed to take in the area.

"We're here to try out some new micro-transmitters. You could be one of the first people in London to get 5G. I'm told that it's so fast it'll make your current games look like relics from the 1980s. I told my boy about it last night, and I swear he went green with envy."

As a fully paid-up teenage boy, Edward preferred to avoid conversation, but this had got his interest. He checked the time and realised he had to get on or he would earn more demerits from school for punctuality.

"5G sounds great. I'd love to stay, but I gotta go."

The man laughed. "Busy, busy. That's the only way to be. This morning is more of a recce really. If all goes well, we'll be back early tomorrow and putting the technology in place. If you have a little more time then, I'd be happy to talk you through it. Who knows? You might even get a head start on your mates."

Edward thanked the man and headed off. His head was full of thoughts about laying waste to his online rivals as they were forced to acknowledge his superior gaming skills.

2

It doesn't take much to reduce London's traffic to a crawl, and Peter Webb found himself caught up in one of those inexplicable journeys that take twice as long as they ought to.

His mood wasn't helped with the arrival of a text from his boss saying he had another meeting, and they would have to reschedule.

By the time he arrived at his desk, he was – he checked his watch – forty-one minutes late. His super-efficient PA, Maria, had already opened his post.

A busy morning seamlessly morphed into a demanding afternoon. It wasn't until his late afternoon walk that he remembered he wanted to check with the council to see if anything was going on near his home.

It was too late to ring, so he checked the website instead to discover that nothing was planned, or at least there was no notice of it.

He sighed and returned to his work. At 7pm it was time to call home and let his wife know he was on the way.

He was on the point of hanging up when she added, "Oh, I almost forgot. You may have to park a bit further away. Part of the road has been dug up. According to Edward, it's something to do with 5G internet. He's been talking to the workmen, and they've promised to show him some new bit of technology. He's beside himself with excitement."

The following morning Edward was wide awake when his father came in, but he feigned sleep to avoid conversation. As soon as he heard his dad leave, he was up and ready to go. Looking out of the window, he saw he didn't have to wait. The workmen were already in place - including the friendly man from before.

He grabbed his school gear and dashed outside where his new friend waved him over.

"Follow me. I've got something to show you in that van just down the road."

The workman led Edward to the rear doors of the white panel van and opened them wide. But, when Edward leaned around him, he was puzzled to see a man sitting there, looking at him with a strange expression.

The schoolboy turned to say something but, before he could speak, he was picked up and tossed inside, as though he was little more than a sack of potatoes. As the doors began to close, the man inside backhanded him in the face.

The blow stunned him, and he didn't resist as tape covered his mouth, and a zip lock was used to tie his hands together.

"You need to be a good little boy and keep quiet," the man breathed. Now, I want you to nod if you understand me."

Edward was too stunned to respond. Instead, he just lay there, struggling to breathe through the gap left by the tape. His brain reacted as though he was being choked to death, filling his body with adrenalin. Before he could stop it, his terror was building. The high-pitched keening sounds he heard were coming from his own lips.

Another slap, hard in the face. This time, the man pulled Edward close enough that he could smell his foul breath. It made him gag, triggering another choking bout, and another slap that left his ears ringing.

"I can keep this up all day, you little runt – but I suggest you stop before I slap you silly."

Edward subsided in terror. His captor leaned forward.

"Now cheer up… it's your lucky day – you're going to be appearing on TV."

3

Detective Chief Inspector, Brian Hooley could have sworn that his colleague, Jonathan Roper, had practically purred as he was handed the Interpol file into the Golden Shot gang. The case represented a perfect challenge, having defeated previous investigation teams.

Interpol officers had worked through last night to ensure the file was bang up to date. Just after 5am this morning, the results had been emailed out to a select membership, of which Scotland Yard Commissioner, Julie Mayweather, was one of the most significant recipients.

For the past twelve months, the gang had been operating throughout Europe, kidnapping and murdering prominent citizens from Spain, Germany, France, Holland and Portugal. Just as it was being thought they were trying for a clean sweep of every member of the EU, they had popped up briefly in Russia then headed for the UK.

It had been decided to hand operational control to Scotland Yard with all other countries monitoring their own borders. That Mayweather had the exceptional talents of Hooley and Roper to call upon was a vital part of the decision and tacit acknowledgement that there were no other investigators quite like them. Interpol was coordinating global efforts to track the gang, including input from agencies like the FBI and the NSA.

Mayweather had received the alert at 10pm last night, and she immediately did two things. She activated a strategic task force combining the very best of the officers at her direct command and agents from the major UK intelligence bodies including MI5, MI6 and GCHQ.

The next call was to the two men now sitting in her office. The DCI, a decorated veteran detective, and Roper a unique talent in the crime-fighting world. The pair had arrived with the dawn and since then had been engrossed in the document produced by Interpol.

The Commissioner never failed to be impressed by the way that Roper absorbed information. His eyes seemed to track backwards and forwards with his eyelids flickering as though he was scanning the words directly into his brain.

When it came to photographs or diagrams, his technique changed. He would hold the picture at arms' length, studying it for a moment and then bring his arms towards his face as though he was zooming in.

She knew his methods worked as he boasted the most extraordinary memory which allowed him to operate like a human-computer. One of his less than flattering nicknames was Google. It was meant to imply he was like a machine, but Mayweather knew it was more of a compliment than jealous rivals realised. Using his perfect recall, Roper could take new information, run it alongside previous details and pull out connections that others missed.

Together the two men formed the prosaic sounding, Data Analysis Unit, a deliberately mundane name designed to obscure what they did. The name they had adopted was the Odd Bods. They had a fantastic success rate in the fight against major crime. Time and again, they were the ones who got results when all seemed lost. But now the pressure was on, like never before.

As far as Mayweather was concerned, these two were her best shot. The more daunting the odds, the better they seemed to like it.

And they certainly lived up to the Odd Bods moniker. Roper was a brilliant but maverick man, with a type of autism that allowed him to master details.

His condition also meant he lacked social skills and was better at making enemies than friends. The problem was, he liked to speak the truth, as he saw it, unfiltered. He could never understand why so many people seemed to have an urgent need to take a call on their mobiles when they saw him heading their way.

Hooley, a talented detective in his own right, was one of the few people who could accept Roper, warts and all. He found a way to bring the best out of him while mostly ignoring the worst of his direct conversational style. The DCI took a perverse delight in recalling the most extraordinary remarks. His current favourite was Roper telling him… "If you don't mind me saying so… you look especially overweight today."

There was something in their personalities which clicked. When they worked on a case, the pair raised each other to new heights.

As Mayweather looked out of her window at the fantastic view of the Thames, she had never been more pleased to have them on the case. The Golden Shot gang may have side-stepped everyone so far… she doubted they would do the same with Roper and Hooley.

She was no slouch as a detective herself. Her rise to the top job at the Met had followed a stellar climb through the ranks. Thirty years ago, she had joined as a uniformed officer in a tough part of South London. Multiple promotions followed until she won command of the elite Major Crime Unit with Hooley as her deputy.

They were a tight team, and after she had been promoted, it was widely assumed Hooley would step into her shoes as chief of the MCU. But he had other ideas, asking her permission to set up the Data Unit. The idea being that it would be just Hooley and Roper full-time, bringing in others as needed. It had been a great success, and she was proud of their work

After agreeing the details of the new squad, Mayweather had offered Hooley a big promotion to Commander. He'd declined, insisting high rank would give him a nosebleed. He had even claimed that he should be called the "Chief Odd Bod."

Despite Roper's growing claim to fame his personal style, or lack of it, could present significant challenges. He could wreak havoc with an email, filling the saintliest recipient with murderous rage and reducing the strong-minded to tears. Two days ago, the DCI had told Mayweather about the latest escapade. It concerned a message Roper had sent to the head of building services, Jenny Pritchard. She had brooded about it for three days. On what Hooley later found out was day four, she had seemed to materialise in front of his desk. Dressed in a plain blue dress, she stood with her hands on her hips, her eyes shining with an unnerving intensity. She held his gaze for an uncomfortably long time before speaking. "Thirty-two years," she said. Then she repeated it louder. "Thirty-two years."

Hooley had kept quiet, a sixth sense warning him to let her say her piece. Caught in her laser-like gaze, he hadn't noticed the document she was holding in her right hand until she waved it menacingly in his face.

"I have been working here for thirty-two years and never once has my work been denigrated in such a fashion. Well, I won't put up with it."

With that, she tore the piece of paper into tiny little pieces which cascaded down on his desk. Then she turned to leave – just as Roper appeared with coffee. "He's the one," she said, "but everyone knows you have responsibility for him."

She marched out with her head held high as Hooley picked his jaw up from the desk. He looked at Roper.

"That was Jenny Pritchard, head of Building Services."

"I know that."

"She was cross – no, the word cross doesn't do it justice. She was furious, beside herself, really, really angry."

Roper seemed uninterested. "I didn't notice."

Hooley sighed.

"Did you send her an email?"

Roper nodded vigorously. "I did. One of my desk drawers is loose and needs fixing."

Hooley had a nasty feeling about this. "What happened next?"

"She sent me a reply saying it wasn't urgent."

"So what did you do then?"

"I wrote back to her."

More silence.

"Did you explain how important it was that she responds immediately and maybe make some suggestions about how she could improve the operation of her department?"

Roper took a breath. He looked genuinely impressed. "How did you know that? But I was very careful… just like you told me to be when sending out emails.

"I said I didn't expect her to understand why these things matter because she is not a detective. I also said if she needed help in finding a better way to prioritise her work, I would be delighted to help her since it was obvious the system, she was using wasn't very efficient.

"And I was careful to be sympathetic. I said that her problem was something that a lot of older people suffer from when they get set in their ways. Talking to me could help make her life so much better."

Hooley had put his head in his hands.

Mayweather couldn't help smiling as she recalled the story. While she would make sure someone smoothed things over, it had taken her mind off work, albeit briefly.

She was wondering who to put on restoring the woman's pride when one of her senior aides knocked and came in without waiting for an answer. He would only do that if it was very urgent.

"There's been a fresh contact."

4

Liz Webb was a sought-after bookkeeper who did most of her work from home. This morning, she'd been working steadily when her inbox pinged with an incoming message.

She checked to see who it was from and, not recognising the sender, decided to ignore it until she looked again at the subject line. It said, "Edward." Something about it made her go cold, and she tapped to download the content.

The internet had been playing up all morning, something to do with the workmen outside, she assumed; and it took an age to appear. All the time, her sense of unease was growing.

Finally, she had it. It appeared to be a video clip – although all she could see was the back of a white van. The clip started and, within seconds, she was experiencing the kind of nightmare that no mother should ever experience.

The film lasted only a few seconds, but it was long enough to show Edward being picked up and tossed into the back of the van. It was on a loop and played twice more before a man in a yellow smiley mask appeared.

"Do you want to get Eddie home again? Just watch this space."

After a pause, the sinister figure carried on speaking to the camera.

"This message was brought to you by the Golden Shot - a Show To Die For." This was followed by the sound of an audience whooping and shouting.

The only reason Liz Webb didn't drop her phone was that her fingers had curled around the handset in a vice-like grip. From somewhere, she found the strength to call her husband. Fortunately, he picked up straight away.

She was beyond coherence.

"Edward, it's Edward. They've got Edward. They've got my boy." She was incoherent and sobbing into the phone, continually repeating her son's name.

Peter Webb felt as though he had been punched in the stomach. Something terrible had happened, obviously. She seemed to be suggesting he had been taken, but who were this "they" who had taken him. It sounded like she knew who it was.

"Liz, please, I can't understand what you are saying. Who's taken him? How do you know he's been taken?"

There was a pause as she blew her nose, then came words that made him feel like he was having a heart attack.

"He's been taken by the Golden Shot. Just get here."

He wasn't big on following news, but he was aware of that story. He recalled they had murdered people in Russia recently. How could his son be involved in any of that? But he did understand that Edward had been taken. He rushed straight home, jumping three red lights on the way. Apart from a couple of holes in the road, there was no sign of the workmen. By the time he walked into the house, his wife had become almost catatonic; he had to prise the phone from her hand so he could see the message for himself.

Within minutes of Webb calling 999, Hooley and Roper were studying the video, at the same time as police in Kensington were on their way to his home. Mayweather had requested her office receive an alert whenever Golden Shot calls came in. This one didn't need analyzing before it was passed straight through.

By the time Hooley and Roper had studied the clip, a car was waiting to take them to Webb's home. Mayweather had a strong team around her who understood when it was time to move fast. Getting their top investigators to the scene was exactly what the system was meant to do.

As the unmarked car sped west, the two men were both processing the information. It seemed a significant escalation since no child had ever before been taken.

The DCI's expression was fierce, his anger genuine at the way a teenage boy was being used in such a way. Hooley might have been estranged from his own family after a messy divorce. Still he could remember his children at this age as if it was yesterday.

He was startled as his mobile rang. Mayweather was on the line.

"I've got the locals in Kensington going house to house, but residents may not be around at this time of day. It might take a big push tonight and early tomorrow morning before we get anything meaningful."

She was trying to anticipate the questions that would soon be flying her way.

"We're starting to get some sense of what happened from talking to the father. He's just about holding it together, so I've personally told the duty Inspector to hold off from anymore questioning until you get there.

"But from what we know so far, this was pretty brazen. A gang of men turned up yesterday and started digging holes. This is London, so no one took any notice, apart, rather ironically, from Mr Webb and his son."

Hooley felt a familiar sense of anticipation as he listened to his boss. "I think you would have to say it was serendipity, you asking us here today, to take over the investigation."

He looked at Roper. "Anything you want to add at this stage?"

The younger man took a deep breath. “This is a clear change in the way they operate. A change that suggests they have stepped up the pace… meaning we don’t have much time at all.”

5

Even with blue lights and a siren, the journey from Westminster to Kensington was stop-start as their car, a dark blue BMW 5 series saloon, kept running into snarl-ups. Sitting in the back with Roper, the DCI was starting to feel queasy, the jerkiness of the journey making him wish he hadn't put quite so much milk on his breakfast cereal.

To his relief, the traffic suddenly opened up, and soon, they arrived at Launceston Place, where picking out the Webb family home was easy. A uniformed PC was standing guard at the top of the steps and, irritatingly, a couple of journalists were lurking nearby. Hooley wondered how they had moved so quickly, then remembered that the Daily Mail was based somewhere in Kensington.

Some cops quite like the Press, some don't. Hooley belonged in the latter group. "The reptiles are already here," he said to Roper, who was clearly set to leap out of the car the moment it stopped, "so watch yourself." Hooley had hoped they'd have a moment to discuss strategy first, but they could hardly do that with eager hacks listening in.

Ignoring the chorus of questions that came their way… "Is it the Golden Shot gang?" They walked up the steps and gained admittance.

The wide hallway had dark, polished floorboards. The wood looked as though it might well have been put down when the house was built. Everywhere the DCI looked, the house was filled with light. It made for an unsettling contrast with the reason they were here. Hooley couldn't resist a shiver as he imagined the aching distress of the parents. He'd spoken to too many people caught up in these sorts of terrible incidents to believe it could be any other way.

Hooley and Roper found the pair in a room at the back of the house, overlooking a tiny garden so that no-one on the street could catch a glimpse of them. Nothing could disguise their sense of desperation. They sat in a pair of matching wing-back chairs, the mother was leaning back in her seat, her face chalk-white and blotchy. Her eyelids and nose were red and swollen from crying, and she was clutching a tissue she was using to dab at her face. Beside her, a glass of water sat untouched on a small table. She was wearing a grey cardigan over a white blouse. Judging by the lumpy look of the sleeves, this was how she was dealing with the used-up tissues.

As they stepped closer, Mrs Webb let out a long breath and leaned backwards, crossing her hands over her breasts. The DCI shivered again, for the thought had come to him that this was how she might look if laid out in a coffin. He silently rebuked himself – all that time spent with Roper was putting a fire under his imagination – and studied the father instead. Peter Webb was leaning forward, right on the edge of his seat. The way he was clenching and unclenching his hands a visual clue to the tension he was under.

Despite his natural empathy, the DCI was determined that he wouldn't let emotion get in the way. His job was to protect this family to the best of ability, and that meant keeping cool. He made the introductions, noting there was no sign of a family liaison officer. He made a mental note to get that chased up; these were people who were going to need a lot of support.

As the DCI introduced Roper, the father made a lacklustre attempt to show any interest. He even offered to make them tea, which they declined.

The DCI began to gently probe. "We appreciate this is a terrible time for you, so just tell us what you can," he began. "anything that strikes you as important?"

Peter Webb made a visible effort to rally, gripping the arms of the chair to anchor himself in place. "I will do anything to get Edward back." He spoke quietly but firmly, nodding to emphasise each word.

Up to now, Roper had been careful to allow Hooley to lead, not wanting to misread the situation and create confusion. But now, unable to restrain his enthusiasm to get information, he felt emboldened to jump in.

"When did you get the first email? And have you had anything since?"

Peter Webb replied, "My wife got it about two hours ago. That's all we've had so far, but I know what to expect next. I've been reading about this "Golden Shot" TV show in the papers. I must admit that, until now, I'd thought it was barely credible, that it would turn out to be some sort of prank by his friends. How my son has got involved, defies belief." He looked at them both, his eyes shining, pleading to be told that it was all just a big misunderstanding. "I don't understand how anyone could pay to watch people being murdered. It's inhumane. It's barbaric. Things like that don't happen in our family, they just don't. We're ordinary people. Not special. We just want to get on with our lives."

As the last word petered away, he started crying, and the DCI noticed that his wife was hugging herself even tighter. As much as the detectives needed information, they were going to have to do this very carefully and gently. Both of the Webbs' were hanging by a thread.

The father sagged, his shoulders slumping. Then he gathered himself.

"I'm sorry. This is tough for my wife and me, but it must be harder for our son. I will be OK. Asking questions won't make any difference to how we feel, and maybe we know something. Please, ask away."

Under gentle probing, it emerged Mr Webb had done some detective work of his own.

"Those workmen did it. I checked with the council, and they never gave permission for the road outside to be dug up. Edward told his mother he'd spoken to the men and they told him they were working on 5G transmitters – but when I checked with the council, there was nothing like that scheduled to be going on. It was all made up. When I rang his school, they said they got a call from his mum to say he was ill and wouldn't be in today. The call came in early. The Head told me it was before 8am, so no-one at the school raised the alarm. I can't believe they were callous enough to impersonate his mother."

Hooley thought impersonation was the least of their crimes but kept that to himself.

Roper spoke again. "That is good information. It helps confirm the time frame, which might prove crucial. We are waiting to get the results of the CCTV around your area from the footage captured by nearby cameras. We expect it will show Edward was grabbed once he left the house. Your information from the school, about the early telephone call, adds more weight to that theory. They wouldn't have made that call until they had him. Now we have a workable time frame… and time is going to be really important."

Mr Webb's face flickered with what might have been the beginnings of a smile, but he quickly sank back into himself. The two detectives tried for more but, after ten minutes of questions, realised they would get nothing more from the parents, at least for now.

The one thing they did have was Webb's work details. Roper was eager to get there, to talk to colleagues and study the layout – but, as Hooley told the couple of their plans, Roper stopped dead and slowly turned back to the parents.

"You need to prepare yourself to receive another email. If I am right, then it will most likely come later today or even tomorrow. My guess is that it will be sent to you this evening, so keep your phone by you all the time."

"What will be in it?" Mrs Webb asked, her voice barely above a whisper.

"They haven't set out their demands. I think they will tell you exactly what they want."

The father went to say something, but Roper cut him off. "You are wondering if you will be able to talk to your son and the answer is no. They will show you a film clip, but that is all you will get. Nor will they allow you to speak to the kidnappers directly. You will get instructions about what is wanted from you, and then, you will have to wait for them to get in touch again."

Peter Webb blinked at him; he had gone grey. "I'm not sure I understand."

Hooley cut in. He knew the pressure was stopping the father from thinking clearly, and he didn't want this to drag on. He could also sense Roper was getting impatient. "Your son's kidnappers, Mr Webb. They need to tell you what they want you to do – and that means how much money they want for your son. These early hours are critical to how we respond to that."

If anything, Webb looked even more anxious. "I thought the police advice was never to negotiate with criminals. Not that we have much money to start with."

Hooley replied, "That's the official advice for sure. No-one likes the idea that crime pays – but, between us, every case must be judged on its own merits." He paused. "We have to be realistic. We're hardly likely to arrest you if you pay a ransom to get your son back. The most important thing is that you keep us in the loop, so we all know exactly what is going on."

Webb still looked concerned. "I understand, but I meant it when I said we don't have much money." He waved his arm around the room. "Asset rich and cash poor. That's us."

Hooley looked sympathetic. "Let's worry about raising the money when it comes to it. I can't imagine a situation where the money wouldn't be available somehow."

Webb lapsed back into despair, and the two detectives finally made their way out, the DCI making a quick phone call. Ten minutes later, he was glad to be outside. Ignoring a fresh barrage of questions from a now expanding media pack, they clambered into the back of the car.

As they pulled away, the DCI turned to watch his plan fall into place. He knew that a couple of the media team would try and follow them so had arranged for "blockers" to pull out and stop it happening. Launceston Place was a perfect road for this, being narrow enough to make it easy to shut out any pursuit. At least for long enough for them to avoid being followed. The last thing they needed was reporters dogging their footsteps.

He was under no illusion it would delay them for long. Reporters were like the proverbial bad penny; they always appeared where you least wanted it.

The police driver headed swiftly towards East London. In the back Hooley, conscious of Roper's warning

that time was of the essence, was crossing fingers and toes. They badly needed a break – and they needed it now.

6

Peter Webb's office was housed in a boxy-looking construction, in the heart of Shepherd's Bush. It was all black glass cladding with stainless steel highlights. It was quite large but, overshadowed as it was by the massive Westfield Shopping Centre, it looked smaller than it was. Traffic was predictably heavy, but Roper and Hooley made surprisingly good progress. As Westfield loomed in front of them, Hooley gave himself a pat on the back – since his divorce, he had avoided shopping centres. Just thinking about shopping in one, made his head hurt.

On the journey, the DCI tried to engage Roper in conversation. But the younger detective was at his most uncommunicative, barely acknowledging that he was being asked questions, instead, producing a series of non-committal grunts. Hooley realised he would probably have more success talking to his own hand. Taking consolation in the likelihood that Roper was tapping into his Rainbow Spectrum.

The Spectrum was Roper's unique way of processing and assimilating the myriad pieces of information he picked up using his extraordinary observational skills. By accessing his Spectrum, Roper could assemble and order data in a mind mapping process that, in part, seemed to work at a subconscious level. It gave him the ability to place apparently random pieces of information in colour coded groupings. This was the key to his near savant-like ability, allowing him to spot the vital connections that other people missed.

Hooley was the first to admit that he didn't really understand the process. Still, he had long ago abandoned his scepticism. It got results, and that was all he needed to know. The fact that Roper seemed to be engaging with his Spectrum so soon was proof if any were needed, of how desperate things were.

The DCI always treated any investigation as if he was the first detective involved. But the Golden Shot came with a history. It was a horrific show hosted on the Dark Web. It had come to prominence over a year when prominent figures in Germany were taken and murdered live on the internet.

He had read about it, horrified that it was attracting huge audiences, all using the anonymity guaranteed by the web to pay money to have someone killed. The Germans had thrown resources at the case, and even appealed for outside help, but got nowhere. It was the same story when people in other countries were grabbed and killed.

Hooley wasn't daunted, but he knew that global attention would soon be focused on the Odd Bods and questions asked about their suitability for the role. He wasn't worried about their ability to do the job, but it would help keep the dogs off if they could get some forward momentum.

As their driver pulled up outside the building, he turned to Roper. "What do I always say when the going gets tough?"

Roper paused with one foot already on the pavement. "You say, 'the tough get going.' Which I presume in this case means us." He was off and running. This ability to go from a standing start was something Hooley admired and envied in equal measure.

By this time the DCI had his own door open and was making his way to the entrance. Quickening his pace to avoid being left behind, Hooley caught a powerful aroma of roasting coffee from somewhere nearby. It made his mouth water, reminding him he was starving, but there was no time for that now. Pressing the sensation down, he hurried on. Up ahead, Roper pushed his way through a door that swung back into place just as Hooley arrived, forcing the DCI to shoulder his way inside. Emerging into a reception area decorated in shades of grey and black. It was obviously expensive and had been done in the fashion of the moment, but this went straight over the DCI's head; Hooley just thought it was a bit gloomy. He did, however, appreciate the soundproofing which was doing an excellent job of keeping the street sounds out, creating a calm and relaxed interior.

Roper hadn't held back. Already, he was waving his ID at a bewildered-looking receptionist, speaking loudly and slowly in what Hooley thought of as Roper's Englishman abroad tone. "I need you to take me to Mr Webb's office right now."

The puzzlement on the man's face was beginning to be replaced by an irritated expression, and Hooley judged they were seconds from a full-blown row. Swiftly, he stepped up to the desk and put on his best smile, making firm eye contact. Very deliberately, he produced his own ID.

Making sure the man stayed focused on him rather than Roper, he tapped the badge. "Detective Chief Inspector Brian Hooley," he read.

The man bowed his head slightly. "How can I help you, officer?"

He managed to put the emphasis on "you" and pointedly turned away from Roper. The DCI could see his colleague was about to say something and doubted it would be helpful. Holding up a warning hand, he quickly spoke to the receptionist.

"While I am not at liberty to explain why, this is a matter of life and death. My colleague was right when he said we needed to see Mr Webb's office. While I am happy to add the word 'please', I cannot stress enough, that time is of the essence. We have just come from Mr Webb's house. If you've been following the news, you will be aware that he and his wife find themselves in a nightmare."

Before he could find out if this approach was going to work, another man appeared. He was stocky, in his 50s, with metal-framed glasses. With his black suit and dark grey tie, Hooley thought he blended in with the décor.

The new arrival held out his hand. "Gerald Stone. I'm the managing partner. I know what's going on. I have already spoken to Peter. A dreadful business for which he has our deepest sympathy." Mr Stone made an expansive gesture. "Nowhere is off-limits, if it helps to find those responsible. Follow me, I will take you to his office. It's on the top floor, and his PA will be able to help you. This whole business is so awful. The clip of his son being taken has been seen by millions of people. It's gone viral. I really hate the way other people get to look in on private grief like that."

Hooley gave him a quick nod of thanks. The man seemed onside, and that was all that mattered. He also hadn't realised, until Stone had told him how the boy's kidnapping was already being watched on the internet.

The development underlined how right Roper was about them changing the way they operated. Not only had they shifted to the UK, but they were also moving faster. According to the Interpol dossier, previous victims had been held for at least 24 hours before the Golden Shot gang revealed they had them. Whatever the reason for this, it showed Roper was right when he hit the ground running.

There was no time to reflect on things they couldn't control. Gently, but firmly, Hooley pushed Roper towards the lifts before his colleague could say anything to create another problem.

Moments later, the pair stepped out on the fourth floor. Stone leaving them to the care of Webb's PA, Maria Morton, an athletic-looking woman wearing dark trousers and a loose-fitting top which failed to disguise the broadness of her shoulders. Her eyes were red-rimmed, for which she immediately apologised.

"I'm sorry I can't stop crying. Peter - Mr Webb. Such a lovely man and devoted to his family. I can't believe this has happened. To make things worse, we'd just had a sort of argument, our first ever. It feels like fate." She started to sniff loudly and produced a tissue.

Hooley quickly stepped up. "The only people to blame here are the ones who have taken his son. Now, I am Detective Chief Inspector Brian Hooley, and this is my colleague, Jonathan Roper."

They both looked at Roper, who was staring at the ceiling very intently. Hooley had got used to him doing this sort of thing, but he knew people could find it unnerving. He glanced at the PA, but she was too wrapped up in her own misery to take any real notice of what was happening.

Roper broke off from studying the ceiling to direct a question at her. "Have you recently had any security upgrades, new motion detectors? Or maybe you've had a new telephone system fitted? It would have been in the last few weeks, so you should remember." He twisted around and pointed at a small unit on the ceiling that looked a bit like someone had expertly sawed a golf ball in half. "What about that thing?"

She nodded, unfazed by the volley of questions. "A few weeks ago, two men came. They were very efficient and put in that thing you've been looking at."

"What about Mr Webb's office, did they get in there?"

Morton looked very serious.

"Oh, no. Mr Webb was actually out of the office that day. I wouldn't let anyone into his private space unless he told me. Anyway, they didn't ask to go in."

Roper's follow up was instantly snapped out. "Who was responsible for ordering the work? Did you ever let the men out of your sight?"

Morton was starting to look anxious.

"They said the partners wanted the work done because our security system was out of date and vulnerable to being hacked from outside. Mr Webb wasn't there. It was hardly my place to check up on them."

Roper was nodding energetically. "Mr Webb was out, but what about the other partners?"

Now Morton was looking very worried.

"They were all at a big conference at the Savoy Hotel. All the senior people were out that morning."

Roper looked at her very intently. "You need to think hard about this question because I've asked once and I think you gave me the wrong answer. Not intentionally, but you didn't think hard enough… Were they ever working here alone?"

The pale looking woman had been turning a shade of pink, but now bright red spots of colour appeared on her cheeks.

"I did have an upset tummy that day. Most unlike me, but I had to go to the toilet a couple of times while they were here."

Hooley was amazed when he saw Roper stiffen as if this was precisely the answer he expected. There were times when his man was positively spooky.

Roper was ready with his next question. "Did they offer you something to drink or eat? Perhaps when they arrived?"

The DCI suddenly realised where this was going and looked expectantly at Morton. She was gazing at Roper as though he was a magician who had just pulled off a fantastic trick.

"How could you possibly know that?" She looked suspicious. "Did you manage to find some way of looking through that security device you're so interested in?"

Roper shook his head curtly. "Of course not, we've only just got here. But I'm betting you had a nice cup of coffee from them."

She sat on the edge of her desk, clearly needing support. "Yes, I did. They said they'd bought one for a colleague who'd been sent elsewhere at the last minute. The funny thing is, it was exactly what I always order – an Americano, black, no milk. I never order anything else."

She clasped her hand to her mouth and looked in such danger of collapse that Hooley grabbed her arm and led her to her chair.

She sat down and started shaking her head.

"This is all my fault. They could have done anything while I was out of the room."

Hooley spoke to her urgently.

"As I said before, this is not your fault. If my colleague is right, and he probably is, you've been the victim of a very sophisticated scam. These people went to great lengths to find out this information."

Roper interjected, "They may have had you under surveillance. You might need to be careful in case they come back and try and shut you up."

Hooley could hardly believe his ears. He gave him a look that would have made a charging rhino think twice – but Roper remained oblivious. Not so the PA, who had gone sheet white and was holding on grimly to the arms on her chair, looking as though the floor had just opened underneath her.

The DCI said, "My colleague can have an unfortunate turn of phrase. Please don't worry. By the time we get out of here, I will have arranged for you to be protected by uniformed officers. It's just a precaution – but you have seen people who may prove central to this." Hooley hesitated before going on, "We've already got officers on the way here, and we won't go until they arrive. Someone will come and introduce themselves and, for the next couple of days, just to be totally safe, we'll have someone at your side. But honestly, I think the chances of them coming back are vanishingly slim."

Out of the corner of his eye, Hooley saw Roper taking a breath. Judging by his grim expression he was about to voice a protest, or even worse issue another dire warning. So Hooley quickly raised his hand towards him, palm outwards. It was their agreed signal for Roper to remain silent.

Sometimes it even worked.

7

In the time it took to walk out of the building, Roper was already lost in thought, something he could do at the drop of a hat. They got in the back of the waiting car and the DCI directed them back towards Kensington.

With Roper mute, Hooley took the chance to get on the phone and check on progress in assembling the Odd Bods back-up team. A lot of the time, the unit could function as just the pair of them, with some admin support. But this investigation was going to need the assistance of dozens of detectives and uniformed officers, preferably ones with the experience of working significant cases.

First, speaking to Mayweather's support team to get the ball rolling. He was assured the first officers would be seconded within hours.

This was the unglamorous side of policing – making sure that rules were followed, witnesses protected, leads followed up, case notes reviewed. The list of essential tasks went on and on. It was also something about which the DCI was uncompromising. Hooley was a firm believer in the philosophy, that the more hard work you put in, the greater the chances of success. He'd once tried to explain it to Roper using one of his favourite sayings.

"The more you practise, the luckier you get."

With hindsight, it was a mistake. Roper could not get the concept at all, arguing that practice made perfect. They'd agreed to differ.

Early on in his career, Hooley had learned his lesson the hard way, when the sloppy work of his colleagues cost him dear as a guilty man had walked free and gone on to hurt many more victims. From that day, he learned why procedure mattered.

Hooley finished his initial round of calls after ensuring officers would be assigned to the PA, Maria Morton.

Glancing over at Roper, who was still deep in thought; if his half-closed eyes were any clue, Hooley smiled. His colleague was a rare talent and needed support to do his best work. He didn't need to get involved in organising the back-up team.

By the time their driver pulled up outside the Webb home, Hooley was happy the first building blocks were being put in place. He knew this case would not be solely a police operation. He had already asked for help from GCHQ. Needing their expertise to take a look at the security system at Webb's workplace.

Almost a minute had passed since the car had pulled up at their destination. Roper was showing no signs of coming out of his semi-trance, Hooley resisted the temptation to nudge him. Long experience had taught him that there were times when he was best left alone. Right now, Roper seemed on top form, entirely focussed on the case. Hooley might have wished he had been a little gentler with Morton. Still he couldn't deny that he had made some pretty incredible intuitive leaps already. Bruised toes and battered egos were part of the price that needed to be paid. It was Hooley's job to smooth things over and help colleagues realise that there was a method to go with the blunt approach.

He also reminded himself that he needed to be on his game where the wellbeing of Roper himself was concerned. In the early days of their partnership, they had worked on a case that had taken off at a similarly blistering pace. Inevitably, the developments and revelations had slowed down, and that had brought its own problems. With Roper's mind still operating at light-speed, he turned inwards, becoming intensely introspective. Left to his own devices, he could think himself to a standstill. It was a problem easy enough to spot when it happened, Roper just stopped. The trick was recognising it in time and finding a strategy to head it off.

A sense of irony struck the DCI as he came realized he had briefly been lost in thought. It was Roper who snapped him out of it when he said.

"I'm sorry. What did you say?"

The DCI gave a wry smile. He must have been talking out loud – but luckily, he'd been muttering because Roper hadn't been able to hear him clearly.

"I was just wondering when you would rejoin the rest of us. It seems I have my answer," said the DCI. "I assume you're about to tell me that your Rainbow Spectrum is buzzing."

The quizzical expression hardened to puzzlement.

"What do you mean 'rejoin the rest of us'? I've never been away." Roper waved his phone. "You could have called me."

Hooley had no idea what he meant about the phone but knew he didn't want a detailed conversation about it, deftly switching track. "If you don't mind me saying, you've been on excellent form today. What inspired you with all those questions you put to the PA? You were spot on."

Roper shrugged. "It was quite straightforward really, especially with what was in the report we read in Julie's office."

The DCI narrowed his eyes. "Just assume that I can't absorb thousands and thousands of words as quickly as you can, Jonathan."

"Hmm, yes. I always forget how slow you are."

Hooley's dentist had recently told him off for grinding his teeth. He was considering this as his colleague ploughed on.

"It was all spelt out in that report put together by Interpol. For every murder, there is usually another person released."

Hooley interrupted. "Are you talking about the online voting system? In some ways, that is one of the most twisted things."

Roper nodded. "In Holland, where they were taking two people at a time, they started getting people to vote for who lived and who died. Dutch police said it was proving very lucrative and attracting many more viewers. The Golden Shot even put up a detailed guide about how to avoid being identified if you wanted to take part.

"People were paying in Bitcoin, which is untraceable. Interpol believes they have made more than thirty million Euros so far – possibly a lot more. So far, those figures are being kept quiet, so they haven't been in the media coverage."

Hooley held his hands out. "OK. That's an excellent background, but I got the impression you were about to make another point."

"I was, and it is this… these people are painstaking and clearly have a detailed plan of action. That included always getting full background. They make to check the habits of not just victims, but also colleagues, friends and family."

"Once we established that Webb's office was bugged it confirmed they were following their plan. With that sorted, what followed next was a straightforward piece of deductive reasoning. It certainly wouldn't have been beyond your abilities. If you were up to speed on what to look for."

Hooley's face darkened. "Why have a dog and bark yourself?" he muttered.

Roper didn't hear or ignored the barb. He cracked his knuckles, a habit that made Hooley wince.

Oblivious, Roper carried on, "It seemed obvious to me that the kidnappers would try and choose a day when as many people were away as possible. Accountancy companies are often invited to big conferences, often held in hotels, so I asked if that was the case here. As we know… it was."

"OK, I'm impressed," Hooley conceded, "But what made you focus on her coffee?"

"Simple… she had a coffee cup on her desk. I could see that she didn't use milk. Because they do their homework, the gang would have known this and brought along the exact drink she might be tempted by." Roper shrugged. "Did you notice that artisan coffee shop nearby? You must have been able to smell it? She would have used that, and they could easily have watched her ordering so that they knew what she liked. People never vary their coffee orders."

"That was very clever of you, but what if she had she refused the drink?"

"I think they might have taken more direct action. These people will go to any lengths to achieve their goal. You can bet they bought some powerful knockout drug to take her out if she refused the drink. Riskier, but it would get the job done. If they were smart about it, she might not have realised anything was going on. There was a case in New York recently where a legal secretary was knocked out – and when he came around, he was told he must have fainted. It was only a couple of weeks later, when he had a flashback, that the truth came out. Too late, of course. The people responsible were long gone, armed with copies of the documents they'd come for."

Hooley nodded grimly. Roper was right. This gang had shown they were utterly ruthless. It was probably just as well that the PA had accepted the doctored coffee.

Roper reached for the car door handle. "Let's get to the house and talk to Mr and Mrs Webb again. I am quite confident that we won't have long to wait until the gang are in touch.

"We know they are now here, in the UK, but I am confident to say they are also based in London, not just because the boy was grabbed here.

"Up to now, no one has been able to find where they operate from. I think previous investigators have missed the point. It's not that they are brilliant at covering their tracks, it's because victims have been taken in one country while the show is broadcast from another.

"But now I think they are not only choosing victims in London, but they are also based here, which is why they had that film of the boy ready so quickly. It was ready at least 24 hours faster than they normally deliver the video clips."

Hooley wasn't wholly convinced. "Couldn't simple geography explain that. I mean we are a lot smaller than mainland Europe?"

"Yes, yes. I thought about that, but now you're missing the point as well, several points, actually.

"Britain is an island, and that creates issues about moving to other countries, inevitably things slow-down from having to cross either over or under the sea. They would never have been able to prepare that video so quickly.

"Just as importantly, the films they make are very high quality so they must use a lot of technology… the reason they went quiet for a while is that they were moving stuff to a new location. London is probably the least likely place anyone would remark on that type of equipment being moved. They'd be virtually invisible."

Hooley couldn't argue with his reasoning. And not for the first time, reflected that it was a massive advantage that his grasp of details allowed him to make sense of confusion.

"Anything you need to add?"

"There is one thing bothering me. We only know about Edward Webb so far, but the chances are high that they have taken others… they always have done in the past. We won't have long to wait."

8

Roper was striding along, walking at twice the pace of Hooley. Behind him, the DCI resisted the temptation to call out, or even run. Instead, he did his best to move at a more leisurely pace.

Reaching Webb's home was to become aware that it was now the centre of a large mob of the press, all of whom were looking at him expectantly. He blocked out a barrage of questions, vanity forcing him to try and take the steps in a sprightly fashion. Roper, having halted his headlong rush, was holding the door open for him and he was glad to step inside and catch his breath.

He also had questions. "Do you have any thoughts about which areas they might be in? Could it be Edward was taken somewhere central? I haven't seen the results of the security camera checks yet, but maybe we can trace the vehicle through the capital?"

Roper looked surprised. "Of course… you're thinking about that new software GCHQ has come up with? I hadn't got around to thinking about that yet."

"Yes, well, you may have double my brain power – but don't forget I know a thing or two about arresting the bad guys… You find them, I'll nick 'em."

As they stood in the hallway, Hooley could still hear questions being shouted by the reporters. With a massive increase in uniformed police, a once quiet residential area was taking on the hallmarks of a full-blown media circus. Which was the last thing he wanted.

One irritatingly loud voice was shouting out their names.

"Are you in charge now, DCI Hooley? Scotland Yard bringing in the 'Odd Bods' for this one?"

To Hooley's dismay, someone had leaked the squad nickname to the press, triggering numerous articles. Most of them poked fun at the pair – but a few did recognise what a vital role they had in taking on Scotland Yard's most complex cases.

The DCI was relieved to note that Roper was doing an excellent job of shutting out the distraction. The younger man simply wasn't equipped to deal with gangs of journalists yelling at him and had adopted the technique of ignoring them.

Roper had once told Hooley that when they were confronted by a mob of yelling media, the effect was similar to walking into a packed bar. The noise merging into a wall of sound that made it impossible to hear individual voices. The fact was, he couldn't have answered even if he'd wanted to.

The beat bobby guarding the door closed it firmly, not that it did much to drown out the noise of the mob. Hooley led the way to the back of the house to speak to the couple. Mercifully, the outside noise was reduced here.

It was as if the couple hadn't moved, although Mr Webb was slowly unravelling. He looked feverish; eyes too bright and forehead glistening with sweat. With approval, the DCI noted that the family liaison officer was in the middle of serving them tea, whatever crumb of normality could be offered might help a tiny bit. Once they were a bit more organised, he would ask about them being looked over by a doctor.

As the father registered the arrival of the two detectives, a series of emotions flashed over his face. Hope that they had some news. Fear that they might be about to be told the worst. Hooley recognised the reaction. He needed to quickly let them know there were no developments. While assuring them of the scale of the police operation that was trying to bring their son home.

He said, "Nothing solid yet, I'm afraid, but we're redoubling our effort on CCTV. Don't get your hopes up yet – but there might be something specific coming out of that. We also picked up some lines of inquiry from your office. It looks as though they had you under surveillance – but that works two ways as we now know members of the gang must have been inside your office, so maybe we'll find something there. It's something we're chasing hard."

Even though he understood the critical importance of checking cameras, he also understood that this might sound peripheral to the parents. As he watched Mr Webb, he knew it wasn't even close to what he really needed to hear. What little energy he had left seemed to expire as he tried to stand but gave up. Instead, he reached out with his left hand, placing it on her arm. She couldn't respond to the gesture.

Hooley jerked his head at Roper to signal they needed to give them a little personal space. The pair stepped outside and made their way down to the basement kitchen.

The DCI said, "I'd hoped we would be able to talk to Mr Webb in some detail about what we found at his office, but he barely reacted to what I said. I don't think we dare push him at the moment. Are you happy to stay here, at least for the time being?"

Roper nodded vigorously. "We have to be here. Everything I read in that report while we were sitting in Julie Mayweather's office points to them contacting the family again, very soon. It will happen sooner rather than later. We need to be here, and we don't want to waste a moment after they get in touch. Edward is by far the youngest person they have taken so far. I don't need my

Rainbow Spectrum to tell me that development is not good news."

The DCI wasn't going to argue when Roper was on this sort of form. "While we're waiting, I can turbo-charge our efforts on the CCTV search. I don't know how much they've found yet, but we can double, or treble, the number of people checking it. We've got to keep applying pressure."

9

An anguished shout sent the two detectives racing back up the stairs where they found Peter Webb looking as white as a sheet. He was holding out his mobile, his hand trembling. Hooley gently took the device and stared intently at the message displayed on the screen.

"Update coming soon. Visit the Dark Web."

Hooley sensed Roper looking over his shoulder. The message read, he immediately went to his own phone to start the process of accessing the Dark Web, using specialised software he'd pre-loaded. Roper had offered to do the same for Hooley. But the older man was convinced that nothing good would come of him having access to powerful software he didn't understand.

As Roper worked his device, the couple watched him intently. Their expressions showing how desperate they were for any scraps of news about their son and hoping for evidence he was still alive.

For a moment, all was silent. Hooley focused on the parents, his clipped tone conveying the sense of urgency he felt. "We have no control and can't be sure what these people are about to show us. The only thing I would say is that, previously, they have shown no sign of sensitivity. Given that, would you prefer it if we stepped away and checked it before you see it?"

It was Mrs Webb who replied, dismissing the offer. "My imagination is already running riot. We know these people have a track record of showing their victims being murdered, but if we were to look away now, it would be like betraying our son when he needs us most."

Despite her obvious distress, her voice was firm. Never underestimate a mother, the DCI thought to himself, pleased at her show of courage.

The DCI could understand their position but was equally determined about one aspect: If things became unpleasant, he would step in.

"Jonathan can access their site, so now we have to wait. Please let it play through. Anything that comes out could be a vital clue. I know this is going to be an ordeal for you but, remember, you're doing this for your son. That is the only thing that matters."

The minutes dragged by as the parents fought to stay calm, their mounting anxiety betrayed by the way they constantly shifted, unable to get comfortable in their seats. Roper never took his eyes off the tiny screen – although the DCI could spot the tell-tale signs that indicated his formidable powers of concentration were kicking in.

His breathing appeared to have slowed down, and his usually chalk-white complexion had become tinged with a touch of pink. It was his hair that was the big giveaway. Normally unruly, it was now sticking straight up like a character in a comedy film who'd been given a jolt of electricity. In other circumstances, it might have been funny. It wasn't now.

"It's here."

The words seemed to float through the air as both parents sat upright, their bodies stiffening with anticipation. Hooley took a deep breath as Roper walked over, positioning the tiny screen so they could all see it.

For a few more seconds, the screen was blank. Then words started to scroll across.

"The Golden Shot. An Extra Shot."

This was repeated on a loop for another thirty seconds before finally, the screen changed to show a brightly lit stage. A hooded figure sat, unmoving, in the centre. The Webbs gasped, assuming they were looking at their son. Then, bounding onto stage, came the smiley clown "presenter".

He ran to the front and shouted out loudly:

"What have we got?"

From the darkness, the crowd shouted back:

"The Golden Shot!"

"What is it?"

"A show to die for!"

"I can't hear you!" Clown Face was cupping his hands to his ears.

The decibels shot up. "A SHOW TO DIE FOR!"

The whoops and hollers took longer to stop, and Clown Face milked it for all it was worth, leaping around the stage and waving his arms wildly in a way that felt menacing and sinister. Hooley felt a near physical urge to put his hands around the man's throat. His palms itched as he looked at the effect it was having on the already panic-stricken parents. He didn't know how they were coping.

Meanwhile, Clown Face was talking again.

"Here at the Golden Shot, we like to make sure everyone gets their money's worth – so today I am bringing you a special preview of upcoming events. I think you will find it all very exciting."

More shouts emerged from the dark as the clown walked across the stage and up to the hooded figure.

"Want to see who we've got under there?"

"Show us!" The crowd was close to hysteria. Their yells grew shriller as the clown grabbed the bottom of the mask in both hands. "Three… two… one!"

The countdown was bellowed out as the hood was whipped away to reveal a terrified looking woman, aged in her mid-twenties. She had dyed blonde hair, a curvy figure and was wearing tight blue jeans and a pink t-shirt. She had a tattoo on her right arm and was wearing glasses with a bright blue frame. Her eyes, shut tight against the sudden glare, were leaking tears.

"Surprise!" yelled the clown, hamming it up for all his worth.

At Launceston Place, the silence was broken by Hooley.

"Who the bloody hell is that?" he asked.

The clown looked up and spoke straight into the camera.

"Wouldn't you like to know?" If a clown could leer, this one was leering.

The shock of the unexpected interaction felt like a physical blow to Hooley, making him step back as though he'd been pushed. Roper had gone rigid, his gaze locked on the screen.

The clown held his hands up.

"Let's give our special welcome to our surprise guests – at least this is a surprise to them. Detective Chief Inspector Brian Hooley and his sidekick, Jonathan Roper."

The audience wasted no time in launching into boos, jeers and catcalls. The clown waved his hands for calm.

"Don't be strangers, you two!" He stared into the camera, then the screen went blank.

In the Webbs' house, Roper and Hooley stared at each other as they both had the same thought.

"They're watching us," said Roper.

10

It took a GCHQ team to find them. State of the art surveillance equipment was embedded throughout the house, inside the television. And even, to the dismay of the couple – in the bathrooms.

Meanwhile, Roper and the DCI had been rushed back to New Scotland Yard for a crisis meeting with the Commissioner. They arrived to find the new head of MI5, Jenny Roberts, already there and waiting. The media and assorted politicians were going mad, demanding answers and speculating about what this meant. At present, the view among the journalists was that the police, with Roper and Hooley to the fore, were being made to look foolish by the kidnappers who were running rings around them.

Mayweather and Roberts – who was in her late 40s and with light brown hair and sharp eyes that hinted at her intelligence, were waiting for the two detectives. Hooley was seething, the short journey merely amplifying his anger, so much so, his boss urged him to sit down and take a few breaths.

Mayweather stood in front of him, hands lightly on hips. "We need to accept they caught us cold and move on. I don't want to get sucked into playing some game of one-upmanship with these people. For all their trickery, they're just criminals, nothing else. It's our job to catch them and make sure they go to prison."

Hooley calmed down; he knew she was making sense. He gave her a rueful look. "Thanks for that, I let the shock get to me. I see we're being called idiots by the press

– but it's not the first time and won't be the last. As you say, we need to catch these people, not win approval from a bunch of hacks." He was glad to see Roper was also relaxing, his deep frown lines smoothing out.

Mayweather inclined her head.

"I've spoken to the Chief of Staff at Downing Street. We've decided that, for now, Jenny and I will do a series of interviews on this. Jenny never goes public, so that should keep them quiet for a bit. The hope is we can keep some of the focus off you – although I doubt it will last for long, not with the media scenting your blood. We'll have to try and remind everyone this is about life and death, not some meaningless point-scoring. I'm hoping we can buy you a small window, but if not, to hell with them, we've got a case to solve."

As usual, it was Roper who was the first to move on.

"Have we discovered who the woman is?"

Mayweather checked her messages. "She's a Welsh reality TV star, Daisy Daffodil… which has to be a stage name, surely?"

To her surprise, Roper nodded. "She's incredibly popular on social media, but no-one even knew she'd been grabbed until she turned up on TV."

He added. "Where was she taken from?"

"She was staying in a hotel in central London."

"When was the last time she was seen?"

"At the moment, the last sighting of her was by the waiter who brought her room service at 8pm last night."

Absorbing the answers at the same speed he asked the questions, Roper looked down at his shoes then back up at Hooley.

"We now have more evidence that my theory over the time frame speeding up is right."

Mayweather glanced inquiringly at the DCI. He said. "Jonathan was working on the theory that the speed with which the gang announced they had taken the boy suggested that they had moved into London. If this Daisy Daffodil was taken this morning, her appearance on the Golden Shot suggests she's also being held somewhere in London."

Jenny Roberts gave Roper an appraising look. She'd only recently been appointed as head of MI5, so she hadn't met Roper before. It was a good job; his reputation proceeded him. With his hair sticking up and his skinny fit black suit, she thought there was a vague resemblance to Oliver Hardy.

"That's very astute of you, Mr Roper. My people have been on this for weeks. Their best estimate was that the Golden Shot was coming from somewhere in France, close to the coast. We think they were in Moscow for a month before that. They will be updating now, but your suggestion sounds right."

She pulled out her mobile and sent a message. Hooley didn't ask but guessed it was to her team.

Mayweather asked, "Do you two have an opinion about why they made such a big fuss over dragging you two into this? Do we think it likely they anticipated you would get involved and the cameras they planted confirmed it?"

Hooley tugged his ear lobe. "You may be right. I do think it's a clear challenge. They want to turn this into some sort of competition, I guess."

Roper nodded. "I think that's exactly what it's about. but I also think that's what they want us to think."

The three of them looked at him expectantly. Despite the seriousness of the situation, Roberts was enjoying herself. She'd heard Roper was the King of Enigma and it looked like that briefing was spot on.

Roper took his time before elaborating. "It won't have been hard for them to work out that Brian and I would be involved. Cases like this are always assigned to major crime teams. From the videos they have released so far, especially the ones with that clown in, British people are playing a big part. I have analysed the clown's voice, and there is a touch of East Anglia in there, overlaid with a London accent. You couldn't fake that."

"How did you analyse the way someone speaks?" asked Mayweather. "Is there some software for that?"

Roper shook his head. "I memorised a lot of accents after I listened to a lecture about the science behind Speech and Language. I wanted to find out more about communication."

Mayweather gave him an appraising look. "So, you can do in your head what everybody else would need a load of technology to achieve?"

Roper shrugged. "I hadn't really thought of it like that. I just do it."

He carried on. "It is self-evident that no police force, anywhere, has managed to achieve anything. So, it would be a reasonable guess by them that Scotland Yard would have the same problem.

Given that Julie is known for being willing to try different options, it's not difficult to imagine that she would turn to Brian and me. As she said in that interview with the Financial Times, 'when all else fails, try the Odd Bods." He then surprised his audience by performing a small bow before adding, "The surveillance cameras at Webb's home would have given them all the confirmation they needed. Brian and I have been in a lot of stories over the past six months or so. The American magazine, People, had us on the front cover under the heading 'Scotland Yard's Finest'."

He stopped talking for a minute as he tried to marshal his thoughts. Roberts found it riveting. She could practically hear the cogs turning in Roper's head.

Roper carried on, "We already know they are meticulous planners so, if they wanted to engage with us, they would have put some thought into it. I think that, maybe, that is why they have come to London – actually, they may even have started here before going on a European tour, so we need to think about that." Roper paused as he formulated one last thought. "Brian is quite right when he says that they are making it personal. But my Rainbow Spectrum says there is more to it than that. I suspect that they need to keep us on the back foot and the kidnapping, coupled with the challenge certainly do.

"But a part of me is wondering if they have another reason. Maybe they have made a mistake and don't want us to spot it because it would give clues about who we are up against."

Mayweather let out a long breath.

"That's a very complicated theory, Jonathan. I'm not saying you're wrong, but have you got anything beyond your suspicions we are looking at it?" She paused. "I'm not knocking your theory, heavens knows you have been proven right often enough, to get my backing. I will make sure that all the other teams on this, consider your 'fatal flaw' theory as well."

Roper shrugged. "I can only tell you what I think. If I am right, then they are unusual criminals because it means they have planned for failure as well as success."

The Commissioner was about to speak when there was a knock at the door. Which opened to reveal her senior aide.

"Apologies for barging in – but you all need to know Mr Webb's PA has gone missing. The protection officer you requested arrived thirty minutes ago, and when he couldn't find her, raised the alarm."

Roper looked like he'd been prodded with a stick. "Do you have any news about that receptionist? Is he around?"

The man looked impressed.

"He's disappeared as well. How did you know?"

Roper was clearly angry with himself.

"I've just remembered that he had his ID badge on upside down. I didn't think about it at the time, but I should have. It's an obvious sign that something wasn't right."

Hooley wasn't letting him get away with that. "Don't be too hard on yourself, Jonathan. No-one thinks you should have made that connection from an upside-down badge; he might have been a sloppy dresser."

Roper wasn't going to be mollified.

"I'm supposed to think of these things all the time."

Mayweather interjected, "I agree with Brian, you couldn't have known. But I do know, I'm not too fond of the way this is going. From now on, you two are going to have armed guards at all times."

11

Roper was determined to get back to Webb's workplace, Stone and Partners. Although Hooley wasn't sure what benefit would come from a second visit so quickly – but they weren't going anywhere until the armed protection team was in place.

The DCI grumbled about the delay but knew that you couldn't just pull specialist officers out of thin air. He had thought to suggest they could manage without the protection but could see from Mayweather's expression that resisting the idea would be a waste of energy.

For her part, the Commissioner used the time to emphasise to the two men why they needed to take their security seriously.

"It's been a very long time since the badge, or uniform, was all the protection you needed. I don't want any of my officers walking into a situation where they could get hurt – least of all you two."

She wasn't entirely sure that either of them was buying the argument, but at least she had tried. To get through to them at all was a tough ask. They were both like a dog with a bone when it came to investigations.

Finally, they were on their way, sitting in the back of a police Range Rover with two uniformed, armed officers in the front. On arrival at Shepherd's Bush, they were made to wait in the vehicle as one of their guards carefully scanned the area. Roper was squirming with impatience but didn't try to argue against orders.

Back inside the office building, they were met once again by a nervous-looking Gerald Stone.

"I have to warn you both that I am taking this very seriously indeed," he immediately said. "You've managed to have a member of staff snatched away while your people were working here. Frankly, that doesn't say much about your level of competence. And what about the safety of the rest of us here? Are we in danger? With the Keystone Cops in charge, we most certainly aren't."

Hooley narrowed his eyes but said nothing. A lot of what the man was saying was driven by understandable fear. Plus, he did have a point. When he said that the PA had been snatched away from under their noses. He was going to have to tread very carefully.

"I can only imagine the stress you must be feeling, sir – and you have every right to pursue a complaint if you wish. At the same time, this is an ongoing investigation. So I hope that you can find a way to work with us to try and get these victims back to their families as soon as possible."

Hooley was pleased to see his remarks strike home as a chastened expression flashed across Gerald Stone's face. Sweating profusely, he produced a handkerchief from somewhere inside his expensive Saville Row suit and mopped at his forehead.

"Can you tell me the name of the receptionist and how long he and Maria Morton have been working here?" Roper began.

Stone replied confidently. "Miss Morton is one of the stalwarts here. She's been with us for around five years. I would have to check our records to be totally accurate." He looked uncertain how to go on. "Gentlemen, I need to check with my office about the receptionist. Please give me a moment." He pulled his mobile from another pocket in his suit, muttering rapidly when it was answered. Then, with an underlying sense of anxiety, he returned his gaze to Hooley and Roper. "He's only been with us for six weeks actually. His name is Ian Henderson. He did seem… very efficient."

Roper was giving him a very intense look.

"Did you do any background checks on him? I imagine your company can have access to some very sensitive information, and you wouldn't want people with criminal records working here."

"Every employee, no matter at what level or capacity, is thoroughly vetted."

Hooley pounced. "What my colleague asked, Mr Stone, was, if *this* man, Ian Henderson, had been properly checked?"

Stone was looking at the floor, the bluster knocked out of him.

"There appears to have been a mix up in HR. He had basic references and ID, but we never asked for a Criminal Records check. I can't explain why. Our procedures are normally very robust."

"You probably didn't think that a receptionist was all that important," said Roper. "It's a mistake that a lot of companies make. But, even so, I'd like to speak to the person in HR who was responsible."

Hooley couldn't agree more. "Mr Stone, would it be a terrible inconvenience to speak to your HR person right now? Maybe they have some vital information."

Stone, who had lost his air of bluster, was back on his phone. A few moments later, the colour drained from his face.

"How long ago was this?"

He listened to the reply, then clicked off and turned to the two detectives.

"I'm afraid the lady concerned became unwell and had to go home at lunchtime."

Hooley rolled his eyes and barked. "Name and address."

Stone looked puzzled.

Hooley used his patient voice. "What is her name and where does she live?" he demanded.

A few minutes later, Hooley was arranging for detectives to make an urgent visit to the address in Uxbridge, a few miles to the West of London.

A chastened Stone was looking to make amends for his earlier behaviour.

"Would you like me to get someone to bring down any paperwork related to Mr Henderson?"

The DCI nodded, but Roper shrugged.

"I doubt if that is his real name. He was obviously planted here by the kidnap gang to help with the planning and execution. The more important question is, why did they take Miss Morton? She doesn't fit the profile of those who have been kidnapped so far. According to my checks, she doesn't come from a rich background and lives in a council house with her parents." Roper paused, weighing these thoughts up. "So, if money isn't behind her being taken, it has to be something else. I think she must have seen something, or someone, that would help us find the gang. Either they have made another mistake, or this is where they made the mistake they are trying to cover up."

Stone was looking at him with a growing sense of respect.

"If you need to talk to any of my staff, including me, we're all available for you. Perhaps someone else saw something that might help you make some progress?"

Roper shook his head. "If they thought anyone else saw something, they would have taken them already. That's probably what the man calling himself Ian Henderson was here for. If I'm right, then he was their 'cleaner' – the man who sorts out the mess and cleans up. It would have been his job to grab anyone who might be a problem and get them out. I just hope we have a chance of saving Miss

Morton, because I really can't see that she has any value for the gang... not alive."

The accountancy chief looked shocked as the words hung in the air.

12

A steady diet of playing video games had given Edward Webb a surprisingly strong sense of time passing. To the extent that he was able to judge it reasonably accurately. Even though his abductors had stripped him of all his tech, they couldn't do anything about the internal clock running in his head. The van had been on a stop-start journey through London for an estimated twenty minutes. Then he had the brief sensation of heading underground before it stopped.

For a time, he was left in silence. Then the rear door cracked open. He tried to see where he was, but the area was in darkness. Grabbed by the arms, he found himself being pulled roughly out of the van – where a sack smelling of mildew was placed over his head.

The hand gripping his left arm tightened painfully and a voice – it sounded like the man from the back of the van – warned him not to "play any games." This was underlined by fingers digging into his bicep, making him cry out.

The voice spoke loudly into his ear, frightening him still further. "We're going for a short walk. If I tell you to do something, you do it. Got it?"

Edward nodded silently and was rewarded with a sharp dig again. "I said – got it?"

Despite his terror, he realised he needed to reply and mumbled, "Yes…"

The response clearly worked, Edward was pulled around and ordered to start "walking slowly ahead." Despite the sack, he was sure they were in some sort of basement. A little further on, he was told to slow down and then guided through a door.

This was repeated twice more before his attacker told him. "You need to be very careful with the next bit. We're about to go down a flight of steps, and I'm sure you don't want to go down headfirst. You'd break your pretty little neck. So, go slow."

The guiding hand suddenly vanished; his mouth went dry as he imagined that one false move could kill him. He pushed his right foot forward; it dangled in mid-air as he sought the next step down. His fear built as he wondered if he was actually above a huge hole that he was about to be thrown in to.

Until now, Edward had thought he suffered from mild claustrophobia. Currently, he was experiencing an acute attack. His heart was hammering, and he was sweating profusely. Unable to go down, he started to back away.

Out of nowhere, a punch landed in his stomach, driving the air from his lungs and leaving him gasping. If the hand hadn't grabbed him again, he would have fallen.

Before he could regain his equilibrium, he was pressed against a cold, solid wall.

"You must be a slow learner. I keep having to slap you. If I have to do it again, you're not going to like it. Now make your way down the stairs on your own – or do you want me to throw you down?"

Through his misery, he replied, "I'll do it."

Somehow, Edward made it, despite finding it the most terrifying thing that had happened so far. Every single step was an agony of reaching out and waiting to make contact with something that would take his weight. He was literally stepping into darkness. The seconds between each movement made him wonder if this was when he was going to fall.

The journey felt like it was taking forever, his thigh muscles burning from the tension he was placing on his trailing leg. Finally, he reached what he thought was the end and started to relax.

"Not yet, sunshine. We're about half-way. You're on a sort of landing." Edward was pulled a short distance, and here he was told that the next flight of steps began.

Going down was as bad as before. He reached the bottom, almost sinking to his knees in relief that the ordeal was over. As he calmed down, he became aware of a cold and wet feeling around his groin and realised, to his shame, that he must have lost control of his bladder.

He was about to sag entirely to the floor when the voice startled him again.

"Take the bag off."

For a moment, he panicked. What if the only thing protecting him was because he couldn't see anything? He realised he was hesitating and quickly pulled it off. Although the lighting was dim, it was still bright after the darkness.

He blinked away tears and finally, his vision returned. Not that it really helped. He was in what seemed to be a large, underground room. It was cold and, to his right, he could see a pair of doors.

"The one on the right has got a bed in it and some blankets. If you know what's good for you, stay in there until I call you. The door on the left is a bathroom with a water tap."

As he was shoved towards the doors, he nearly stumbled. Regathering himself, he opened the door. The idea of lying down under some blankets was suddenly appealing. The room was in darkness, so he made his way inside carefully.

"The beds on your left."

With the door closed, he edged carefully forward until his leg was against what he assumed was the bed. With more fumbling, he got hold of the blankets and pulled them aside before lowering himself onto the mattress.

Waves of exhaustion spread through his body, he had never felt so afraid in his life. But after his ordeal, the bed and the blankets were proving an irresistible draw. He tried to fight against the urge to close his eyes, but all he wanted to do was sleep: just shut his eyes for a moment and regain his composure. He finally began to sink into the embrace of the bed. At home, he would have refused to lie on such a thin, damp and smelly mattress. His head was swimming; he couldn't resist the urge to fall asleep.

He was almost gone when it felt like an icy hand gripped his heart.

There was someone, or something, in the room with him.

13

The search for Maria Morton had proved short-lived. Two hours after an armed team had entered her flat in nearby Acton, she had called in.

She was full of apologies, explaining that she'd taken herself off to the gym for an extra-long workout, where she had met a friend and gone on to have a meal and to talk.

Morton was interviewed by one of the detectives recently assigned to the Odd Bods team, and the taped conversation was being listened to by Hooley and Roper.

"I just wasn't thinking. I'm sorry that I didn't let anyone know." Even on the tape, they could hear the emotion in her voice. She went on. "I really like Peter, he's a lovely man, kind and helpful. I've also met Edward; he's going to be just like his dad. I suddenly felt overwhelmed and needed to get out.

"I do a lot of exercise, so I went to my local gym and really went for it. I can't say I feel better, exactly, but it let me escape for a while. I haven't been able to stop myself thinking about what will happen to Edward at the hands of these animals.

"I hate to admit this, but I have seen the Golden Shot. Someone I know, not a friend exactly, can find things on the Dark Web. It actually made me vomit when I saw what they did to the losers. It was awful, just awful.

"While I was working out, a friend arrived saw that I was in a bad shape, and we went for something to eat. It turned into a long afternoon, just talking.

"I didn't want anything to interrupt that, at least for a few hours, so I turned off my phone. I'm so sorry for any trouble I may have caused."

The DCI listened to the detective telling her not to worry and then asked Roper. "What did you think?"

"Actually, I wanted to ask you a question first."

"Really? How can I help?"

"What did you make of her saying she turned her phone off? I would never do that. But you're always telling me I'm not like other people."

The DCI knew he was being asked a serious question and gave his answer some thought. "First of all, it isn't something I would do either. Like you, I regard the phone as essential, and I am always available. The only time I might switch it off would be at night, when I am trying to sleep… but even then." He made a rocking motion with is hand before carrying on.

"Having said that: Assuming she's telling us the truth, she has had the most appalling shock and that does make us do strange things. As for turning her phone off, my kids are about her age, and it always amazes me how they can drop off the radar without any warning. So, overall, I can understand her turning her phone off."

Roper absorbed this information, blinked and then responded.

"Thank you for telling me that. I didn't know how to place the phone information, but I do now.

"I think she is probably telling the truth, and I can now fit it all together. Let us add her to the list of people who need background checks. I also would be interested to know if she has had any unusual payments going through her accounts."

Hooley nodded. "Good idea. I'll talk to the team back at Victoria."

While the pair had been talking, Julie Mayweather was being driven to see them.

As her driver pulled up in Launceston Place, she delayed getting out as she reflected on how much there was riding on her belief that the unorthodox pair would win this battle. She genuinely wasn't worried about her own position she'd had a great career, and nothing could take that away. But there were lives at stake, and this was a case that was starting to scare civilians… she couldn't have that. Her doubts left her. The die was cast, and there could be no turning back now.

14

Edward Webb tried to make as little noise as possible, but his own breathing sounded loud in his ears. Trying to pinpoint what had activated his sixth sense, he made a determined effort to make himself quieter. Then he heard it again: Faint noises from the darkness. A thrill of fear ran through him as he realised there was somebody here.

Fear induced paranoia made him wonder if this was a trap set by his captor and he tried to keep as still as possible, fighting back an urge to call out. Even with his eyes adjusting to the gloom, he couldn't make out the dimensions of the room or precisely where the noises were coming from.

Keeping as still as possible, he strained his hearing. He finally decided that the noise was being made by a human being and was coming from directly opposite him. He wondered if there was a matching bed against the opposing wall with another victim lying there, as terrified as he was.

Time passed with no way of measuring it, but his senses told him he hadn't been down there for more than half an hour. He realised that whoever it was hadn't moved at all, which finally gave him the courage to do something.

He sat up slowly, deciding that, if he was going to be attacked, he didn't want to be lying down when it happened. Yet, as he picked himself up, his courage started to waver. Terrible pictures of what might happen if he drew attention to himself flashed across his mind. Then, as his nerves got the better of him, he sank back onto the bed.

He stayed still for what he judged was another ten minutes, listening intently to the quiet noises coming from the other side of the room. It was definitely another person – for a moment he had endured a frightening thought it might be an animal – and whoever it was, was doing exactly the same as him: Trying not to attract attention. He lay there for another minute and was suddenly filled with resolve. Sitting up before he faltered, he called out, “Hello. Don’t be afraid. My name’s Edward, and I’m being held captive.”

He sat there in the darkness, his breath coming in shallow gasps as he waited anxiously for a response. At first, there was only silence. Then he heard a quiet mumble.

Straining his ears, he tried to make out what the voice was saying but couldn't distinguish any words. He decided he was going to have to risk speaking again.

“I know you're there,” he ventured. “Please don't be frightened. I was taken outside my house just a few hours ago, so I think we’re in the same situation. I can imagine what you’re going through. My name is Edward. I was on my way to school when they grabbed me from right outside my house.”

His words prompted a response as a quavering voice emerged from the darkness.

“Hello,” a female voice with a Welsh accent answered, “my name is Daisy, Daisy Daffodil. I feel like I've been here forever, but they took me from my hotel in London last night.”

Edward could barely believe his ears. He was sure he knew who this was.

“I hope you don’t mind me asking, but are you *the* Daisy Daffodil? The Passion star?”

He wasn't really a massive fan of most TV programmes, preferring to go online – but, along with every other teenage boy, Edward held a candle for Ms Daffodil. He blushed furiously as he thought of her in one of her trademark tiny bikinis and was suddenly grateful for the darkness.

There were only a few years in age between them, but she might as well have been a creature from another planet, at least as far as he was concerned. His mind boggled at the thought that he was in the same room as her; the pair of them being held captive.

She spoke again, "Do you know why they are holding us?"

He actually did have an idea about that, and it was one he was resolutely trying not to think about because it made no sense. What could the people behind the infamous Golden Shot want with him? Then a nasty thought occurred to him. Daisy certainly had a very high profile, but she was of a type taken so far. Maybe it was his role to add a bit of contrast, the useless schoolboy who had no money?

But now it was getting harder to convince himself that this was all a ghastly misunderstanding.

He decided to play his cards carefully and would wait a while before openly discussing what he thought. Instead, he said, "I'm not sure really. Have you been following the news about this weird game show on the Dark Web, the Golden Shot?"

"Not really," she replied. "I don't really watch anything apart from things that I'm involved in – and, even then, I only look at the stuff my agent suggests or when my mum tells me to have a look."

Peter recalled the latest controversy on Passion Island, and how Daisy Daffodil had been caught in an illicit clinch. Causing her boyfriend to go looking for the other man and threatening to punch him in the nose.

“Er, yes. I think I remember the last time there was a bit of an argument on your show…”

A brief silence was broken by the reality TV star.

“Edward? Would you mind if I asked you for a huge favour?” She ploughed on, not waiting for an answer. “I'm freezing. Could you come over here so that we can lie together and get warm from each other's bodies?”

As the words clunked into place inside his brain, Edward was suddenly giving off enough heat to warm a small town.

He had just had the offer of his life, but it had overwhelmed him with embarrassment. At the same time, a tiny part of him was saying the plan was entirely rational. They would keep each other warm and, if they were going to get through this, they would have to work together.

He started to gather up his blanket when the room was flooded with light. Blinded, Edward looked up to see that the door had opened and someone was shining a powerful flashlight through the door. It was dazzling.

“Edward Webb,” a loud voice called out. “Come with me. You are needed.”

15

The Odd Bods were waiting for Mayweather in the mobile command vehicle, which at least offered them protection from the long lenses of the media pack – who had once again started shouting questions as soon as they saw the investigators arrive.

The vehicle had a tiny conference area at one end, and that was where the trio was now standing.

Julie Mayweather noticed how focused Roper was.

“I've seen that expression before, Jonathan. You look like you’re about to tell us all something.”

Roper pointed at the flatscreen monitors on the wall, which were currently blank. They were linked to the Webbs’ broadband connection, which would allow the officers to see any incoming messages at the same time as Edward’s parents.

“I've been saying to Brian that everything points to them shifting their base of operations to London, and they have done it at some point in the last few days. I don’t think their movements are random, however. They need a well-supplied base of operations so they must have been planning this for months, if not years. At first, it was my Rainbow Spectrum that was showing this – but there is increasing evidence pointing in that direction. I’ve talked about them getting people on air so quickly, but the fact that they are speeding up the pace is interesting. By that I mean they might have tried to cover their tracks a bit, kept the same time frames from kidnap to video, but they’re not doing that. Instead, they are goading Brian and me. That is why I am confident they are in the inner London area. They want to be close-by in every sense."

Before the commissioner had the chance to respond, there was a flurry of activity by the technical staff. On the mobile command vehicle walls, the TV monitors had suddenly come to life with letters and symbols scrolling across the screen.

At first, the letters made no sense. Then it all fell into place.

"Incoming message detected on Mrs Webb's phone."

All eyes now focused on the main screen. A few seconds later, a message appeared.

"If you want more information about your son, make sure you are tuned into the Golden Shot in five minutes. If you don't know how to do that, I'm sure Mr Roper is on hand to help you out."

The message was signed off with a sinister-looking clown face.

Roper showed no reaction to his name being included in the message. It had already become clear that the gang was determined to namecheck him at every opportunity. He could see no point in reacting in any way that played into their hands.

Wanting to get back to the Webbs' house, he started to make his way out of the vehicle when a hand on his arm stopped him. It belonged to the DCI.

"Just before we go, do you have any thoughts for us?" Hooley asked Mayweather.

"Yes," she replied. "I wanted to make sure you had all the back-up you needed. You know how highly I value you, both of you, and I won't have you failing because of a lack of support. I'm old fashioned enough to still like to see things with my own eyes.

"I may not have the same heightened senses as Jonathan, but I can detect when things are coming to a head, so that's why I'm here… to get boots on the ground… smell the coffee, call it what you like. I needed to see for myself. And unless you say otherwise, you're fine."

Hooley patted her arm in a consoling way. He knew she found it tough watching others do the work. All this exchange bypassed Roper, who barely acknowledged her as he left the vehicle, but Hooley said.

"You can tell me to get back in my box, but there is one thing you could consider… do you have the energy to talk to those journalists outside? You know everything – so, if you could come up with some words to keep them quiet, that would be doing me a huge favour."

She smiled. "I've already promised to help out on the media duties front. So now is as good a time as any to start."

As Hooley followed Roper back up the steps, the commissioner strode towards the waiting press pack. Feeling a keen sense of anticipation igniting her body, giving her the charge she would need to stay on her toes and get through the next few minutes. Out of the corner of her eye, she spotted one of her media team going pale as the man realised what she intended. He was almost hopping on the spot with anxiety and, if she hadn't been so busy suppressing a laugh, she might have told him off, for imagining she could have lost her touch.

16

Inside the house, the DCI noted the mounting toll the kidnapping was having on the Webbs. It was always the same for the families of those who had been kidnapped. A sense of helplessness, fear, anger and misery that combined in a toxic cocktail to suck the life out of them. He never failed to be moved by it, and it always made his resolve that much harder.

Roper had moments when he could be surprisingly empathetic. This turned out to be one of them as he knelt by Mrs Webb's chair and placed a hand on her shoulder.

"We are here to see this through with you. Are you ready to watch, or do you want us to watch it for you?"

Mrs Webb shook her head, her response neatly summing up what must have been her dilemma – torn between needing to see her son and frightened at what might have happened to him.

Roper checked the iPad was set up correctly before settling back to wait for the broadcast. He leaned into Mrs Webb in an almost conspiratorial way.

"We have got all the major security services monitoring this, so let's hope they make a mistake which tells us where they are broadcasting from. It's a faint hope, but we will never give up. You need to know that we're trying absolutely everything."

She didn't show any sign of hearing him, having withdrawn into herself to conserve her remaining energy.

Still, Mr Webb managed a tight smile to acknowledge he had heard.

All too soon, there came the familiar blast of drums and trumpets, the discordant intro that accompanied all broadcasts from the Golden Shot team. Evidently, the music was only intended to grab your attention, not win any awards.

As the music came to its explosive end, it was replaced with a fuzzy shot of Edward that slowly moved into focus. Roper was using the full screen of his mobile to show them what was happening. Edward's mother moaned softly but remained very still. The DCI thought the schoolboy looked remarkably composed considering what he was going through. For a few moments, he stood there saying nothing; then he coughed to clear his throat.

"I have to tell you that bids for me will start at one hundred thousand pounds and it is expected that I will cost at least one million pounds, so that is my 'buy now price'. You all know the score."

The screen went blank, and Mrs Webb dissolved into floods of tears. Her husband, who had been standing beside her chair, slowly sank to his knees – as if the weight of the world was suddenly upon his shoulders. He had both hands pressed against his face.

"They always want the money very quickly and in cash. I don't know how I'm going to be able to do that, not in the time available. Even if I could manage the smaller sum, I don't have access to a million pounds."

"Have you spoken to your company yet?" asked the DCI. "Surely they can help you find some way of doing this? As we've said before, it's not really our place to advise you on how you might get the money for a ransom. I suggest you speak to your partners immediately. By the time you see them, they will have seen the video and understand the seriousness."

Something about the DCI's tone seemed to inject some confidence, some sense of purpose, into Webb. Standing up, he looked around, as though surprised to find himself at home, and turned to Hooley.

"You're quite right. We have this house, and my firm will be able to help. I shall make some tea for us all, then go and make the phone calls I should have done earlier." He made it as far as the doorway before spinning around on his feet. "On those TV shows, they always say that kidnapping is a terrible crime because the victim always ends up being murdered anyway. It's just a way of delaying the worst. Do you think that's what is happening here?"

Hooley tried to keep his response as neutral as possible. Webb had just identified the central dilemma when dealing with kidnappers.

"Right now, what we can be certain of is that your son is alive and the people who have taken to him are in contact. They don't seem to be concerned that the police are involved, so we have to take them at face value. I hate to use the phrase 'professional'" – he made quotation marks with his fingers – "but that's what these people are. I think that this is in our favour. It means they want to do business." Hooley paused. Whatever he'd been saying, it seemed to be giving Mr Webb strength. "I have seen more difficult cases than this resolve themselves with the victim being released – so we can take some hope."

17

Hooley and Roper made their way down to the kitchen so that they could speak without being overheard.

"What did you make of all that?" asked the DCI.

Roper leaned back against one of the kitchen units, his arms wrapped tightly around his body – a sure sign he had been deep in thought.

"A lot is changing here. When these people first appeared, just over eighteen months ago, their targets were of a similar type. None of them was especially well known, but they were all very successful and had made a lot of money. Solicitors, bankers, pensions experts – those sorts of people. They could access cash more easily than most or were from families who could get it for them. But we are now moving further from that model by moving to London." Roper paused. "We know they have Daisy Daffodil and now they have Edward Webb as well. So the key question is, why they have done this? Up to now, they have been very successful, but I can only think that these changes may create more problems for them, which is very strange."

The DCI paced around the kitchen while his friend was talking.

"I'm totally with you. I don't need your skills to see that there's something strange going on. The thing I don't understand is why they took this Daisy Daffodil. I share your lack of interest in celebrity TV, and I care even less for the whole celebrity circus. But even I am aware that

Daisy is very popular so I'm thinking that taking her can only ramp up the pressure… on them as much as us."

"Twenty-eight million," said Roper, staring down at his shiny shoes.

"I'm sorry?" said Hooley, who thought this was an exceptionally puzzling response even by Roper's standards.

Roper shook himself as though coming out of a trance.

"Daisy Daffodil has twenty-eight million followers on Instagram. It is a lot, but there are people with more."

The DCI had no interest in social media and would only engage with the concept if it was for work. He knew this was going to be an occasion when he needed to be involved.

"Is that a bit like having Facebook friends?"

Roper nodded. "She has gained another hundred thousand since this morning."

Hooley pulled a face. "That's what I dislike about social media. All these people piling in after something bad happens, isn't that a bit ghoulish?"

"Not really. It's just the same as in the old days when people used to buy newspapers to find out what was going on."

The DCI bit down a snappy response. As far as he was concerned, buying a newspaper could hardly be categorised as 'living in the old days', he had picked up a copy of The Times earlier today. But he knew that Roper was making sense.

"So. what you're trying to tell me is that, if we thought this case was attracting a lot of attention already, then it's just about to go wild?"

Roper looked at him. "It most certainly is – and that's why I think we need to bring in some extra help. I've already sent a text to Susan, and I'm waiting to hear back from her. While it is fair to say that I know more about social media than you do, that really isn't saying very much. Susan, however, really gets it."

The woman he was referring to was Susan Brooker, a brilliant data analyst who was more than a match for Roper in that particular field. She had worked with him on many occasions in the past and was a comfortable fit with the Odd Bod philosophy, frequently finding herself puzzled as to why the rest of the world did not share her enduring fascination with examining thousands of pieces of data to find clues that other people would never have spotted.

Hooley was a confirmed fan and knew what she could bring to the investigation an extra dimension that would complement the work being done by himself and Roper.

"Excellent idea, Jonathan. Remind me, where is she?"

"Not that far away at all. She's currently in Paris with the French Secret Service, helping them reconfigure an AI-controlled data management system and taking the opportunity to improve on her French. I'm expecting to hear from her at any moment. Hopefully, she can join us very soon."

The DCI could feel the beginnings of a nasty little headache building up. It was trying to imagine what AI-controlled data management looked like. He decided not to pursue it.

"Is there anyone else you want to add to the team?" he asked.

Roper shook his head. "There will be, no doubt about that – but for now it might be best for the three of us to work together. After all, we all understand each other."

While Roper was talking, Hooley had walked to the end of the kitchen and was gazing out of the window, without taking in what he was looking at. "I'm really not getting the best feeling about all of this. What about you?

An unfamiliar expression crossed Roper's face. The DCI thought it looked like anxiety. It was never good when Roper felt anxious.

Roper was studying his shoes again. They were shiny enough he could probably see his reflection in them.

“I do – but I need to think about it a little bit more. I don't think you're going to like the answer.”

18

With his blindfold back on, Edward was returned to the holding room. Before he was roughly pushed inside, his unseen captor said, "It seems you *can* get something right. The boss is quite pleased with you – so you and your little friend here, have earned some privileges. Just don't go thinking this means you're in the clear. Any messing about and you bounce straight back to zero."

As the door closed behind him, a dim light came on, and he could see the beds on either side of the room. Even better, he could now make out Daisy Daffodil. The light was far from perfect, but it allowed him to see that she had stayed exactly where she was while he was away. She didn't respond to the improved illumination. Instead, she lay wrapped in her blanket with her eyes pressed shut, hoping that what she couldn't see wouldn't hurt her.

Edward wanted to comfort her but lacked the confidence to do anything. Instead, he moved to sit on his own bed and hoped that she would once again, ask him to help her warm-up. As he wrapped his blanket around his shoulders, he was suddenly overcome with a longing for his mother and fought a losing battle to fight back the tears. Sometime later, finally regaining control, he leaned back against the wall, just as the door opened and someone wearing a hood brought in a tray with food and water.

His stomach started growling at the prospect of something to eat, and he had to stop himself from running at the food and stuffing it in his mouth. Instead, he carefully went over to examine the contents: a couple of cheese sandwiches wrapped in plastic, and two bottles of water.

He called out to Daisy. “There’s something to eat and drink. Have you had anything since they brought you here?”

She didn't answer, but he could see her shake her head.

Realising it was important she took on some fuel, he carefully picked up one of the water bottles and took it over to Daisy.

“You need to drink,” he said. “You mustn’t let yourself get dehydrated, or everything is just going to feel worse than it already is.”

There was no response, so he tentatively reached out to touch her hand. He was shocked at how cold she felt and immediately rushed over to get his own blanket. Placing this on top of her, he cautiously rubbed her back and shoulder in an attempt to warm her up.

After a little while, the attention seemed to get through to her, and she rolled onto her side, opening her eyes to look at him. They were so blue and liquid; he could barely drag his own eyes away. Carefully, he brought the water into her eye-line.

“Here, please. Have something to drink. Then you need to eat. You’re too cold, Daisy. The food will help.”

The desperation in his voice got through to her, and she accepted the plastic bottle, taking a few sips before handing it back.

Encouraged, he went back for the sandwich which he carefully unwrapped, handing half to her.

“I think I need a little more water if I'm going to eat some of this,” she said weakly.

Her words calmed him, and he felt his heart slowing. Only then did he realise how it had been pounding against his chest.

After a few more sips of water, a little colour came back to her face. She tentatively chewed on the sandwich, managing a few small bites before flapping her hand to indicate she had had enough.

"Thank you."

He managed a weak smile of his own.

"If you're sure you've had enough, I might have some myself."

This comment produced a bout of wheezing which worried him until he realised she was laughing.

She spluttered to a stop, wiping her eyes.

"I don't think I've ever met a teenage boy who isn't hungry. Please go ahead. I've had quite enough for now. And don't worry about me – you don't get to look good in a bikini by eating all the sandwiches."

This induced a second round of coughing laughter and, once he had been able to rid himself of the image of her in swimwear, he realised she was mocking herself.

He looked at her with new respect. "You come across as… well a bit scary on the TV – but you don't seem like that at all."

His comment brought a wicked grin. "You mean you think of me as being a bit of a bitch."

He went to protest, but she placed her hand on his.

"Please don't worry about it. In the big world of showbiz, everybody has to have some sort of story. You can't just be yourself. Mine is that I'm angry and quick to attack people – but that's not like me in real life at all. It's just an act." She paused. "I'm not that keen on it really, but I am good at it – and that's what keeps me in the show. But if I didn't have Passion Island, I'd be lucky to have a job at all. The one bit of my story which is true is that I didn't come from money and there really is no work back where I grew up in Wales, so getting the opportunity was just fantastic." She shook her head, suddenly sombre. "I always worried it was too good to be true. Now, this has happened."

Edward couldn't think what to say about this unexpected turn, so he did what fifteen-year-old boys do best; he stayed silent.

After a few minutes, he realised that she had drifted back to sleep. Despite his own hunger, he carefully wrapped the second half of her sandwich, determined to offer it to her when she next awoke.

He was sitting on the floor with his back resting against her bed and his knees drawn up tight against his body, just drifting off to sleep when the door crashed open.

It was the same man from the back of the van from this morning. This time, he was making no attempt to disguise himself as he walked in.

He sneered as he took in the scene.

"Isn't that lovely? Little Miss Daffodil has got herself a knight in shining armour. Shame the best she could conjure up is a bit of a wally who couldn't punch his way out of a paper bag. If it was down to me, I wouldn't want him in charge of protecting me – I wouldn't even leave him in charge of a bag of sweets."

The barbs felt all the more wounding because Edward knew he was a skinny kid who didn't intimidate younger boys, let alone burly adults. Anger and shame made him blush furiously. Against a violent man like this, he didn't stand any chance.

His tormentor crossed the space and grabbed the reality TV star by the wrist, yanking her hard to pull her upright on the bed and onto her feet.

Her eyes wide open in shock, she tried to pull away, but the man slapped her hard. Just bare moments before she'd been lying with her eyes shut. She might even have been asleep, and she pulled against her tormentor.

His response was to yank her harder. “Stop struggling if you know what's best for you.”

He pulled her over to the door and. As he was about to drag her through, he turned to Edward.

“You’re next. Unless you want worse than this… you're going to do exactly what you're told.”

19

Daisy Daffodil's tear-stricken face stared down from the massive monitor at the back of the newly enlarged main investigation room.

In the last forty-eight hours, dozens of officers, detectives and specialist support staff had moved into the space near Victoria station as the Odd Bods investigation moved at a tremendous pace. Many of the officers and security agents had come from other countries having been involved with the earlier investigation teams. They brought a lot of knowledge with them.

The teams from MI5, MI6 and GCHQ tended to stick together. Although Hooley had been very firm that everyone should cooperate, and he was pleased when his Senior Inspector reported that all sides were pulling together.

With the monitor displaying events live, the entire room had come to a halt. Upon the screen, the latest transmission from the Dark Web was being played out.

Edward Webb appeared, dark circles around his eyes highlighted how pale he was. His hair looked greasy and lay against his head. Despite his obvious distress, he sat up straight, looking straight down the camera, presenting a stoical face… Especially for his young age.

He was made to repeat the demands for his ransom, his voice breaking slightly as he did so, refusing to give in to the fear he must have been feeling.

He repeated the ransom demands. "You can pay one million pounds and get me back today." He finished and glanced over to the side where someone was whispering to him just off-camera.

He looked back at the lens.

"They want you to come up with the first hundred thousand pounds as a sign of good faith. I'm to tell you that it isn't very much. Not if you love me. You've got forty-eight hours."

The cynicism of the demand made Hooley's blood boil. He reached for his phone to contact Peter Webb and check on how far he'd got towards raising the money. But, before he was able to dial, Daisy Daffodil appeared on the broadcast.

It was the first time the Golden Shot gang had moved straight from one victim to another. She looked terrible, a long way from her toned and buffed appearances on Passion Island. Instead of a flimsy bikini, she was dressed in a pair of scruffy leggings under a thin T-shirt that did at least conceal most of her body. It was her hair that seemed to have suffered the worst of her captivity. She was famed for her thick, lustrous blonde hair – she claimed to spend three hours a day brushing and combing it to keep it in peak condition – but it was far from perfection right now. It was hanging down in a style that Hooley's mother would have called 'rats tails'. This was a long way from her depiction in the tabloid newspapers as one of the most glamorous women in the world.

But it wasn't her appearance which brought the biggest gasps of shock. It was the words she was forced to read out that stunned the watchers, a hardened group of men and women who thought they had seen it all.

In a quiet voice, she read slowly from a piece of paper held in trembling hands. Occasionally she glanced up at the camera and viewers could see the tears slowly running down her cheeks.

"Some of you may know me. I'm Daisy, out of Passion Island. I'm appearing on the Golden Shot because it's time to do something a bit different.

"My minimum release figure has now been increased to reflect my value on social media. The people with me would like it acknowledged that my profile has been raised considerably since I was taken. They feel it is only fair that they should benefit in kind from what they have done. Thirty minutes ago, my followers on Instagram went to twenty-million, an increase of a million new followers in just over forty-eight hours. This is an exceptional increase and means there is going to be an exceptional price for my freedom. I will need the help of all my friends, family, and above all my fans if the price is going to be met. With these changes in mind, the people holding me feel that the most reasonable figure for my ransom demand is twenty million pounds."

Her picture dissolved before the mocking message "The Golden Shot – A Show To Die For" scrolled across the screen.

In the investigations centre, there was a stunned silence. Then everyone started speaking at once. The figure being demanded was extraordinary.

The shouting started to die down only when everyone realised that Daisy had reappeared and was once again looking down at her briefing notes. In the investigation office, everyone's attention went back to the screen.

Daisy glanced at the camera as if she could see the impact of her words. According to a counter on the right of the screen, more than five million people were watching the live broadcast from the Dark Web.

"The money sounds like a lot because it is a lot, but when you break it down, I am only asking for one pound from each of my followers. That's less than most people spend a week on coffee, so I've been told to ask you if you are willing to let me die for such a tiny amount?"

The Golden Shot credits rolled before the screen went blank.

This time the silence was broken by the DCI, and all eyes swung towards him as he called out.

"Everyone, please. Your attention. We need to put the amount of money to one side. The most important thing here is to make sure that she – and all the other hostages – are returned to their families alive and well." He paused. "I am also going to request an urgent security sweep of this office. As you know, they've already caught Jonathan and me, so why not here too? They've proved themselves audacious and clever planners. It could be they' re watching us right now."

With that, all eyes immediately started scanning the room.

"I think this emphasises how careful we need to be. I know our process is already very robust, and many of you have vastly more experience of cybersecurity than I will ever have. But this is a reminder that the people we are up against are sophisticated, ruthless adversaries."

"Now I'm sure that you will have many thoughts and everyone who wants to will get a say, but first I'd like to hear from Jonathan. What did you make of that?"

Every pair of eyes switched to Roper. In a different place, the attention would have been too much, but as engaged as he was, he barely noticed how many were looking at him.

He spoke slowly, making Hooley think he was still assembling his thoughts as the words came out.

"When Edward Webb started talking, there was a faint trace of water vapour. Did anyone else notice that?"

Most shook their heads, although one woman put her hand up. Hooley had missed it as well, so intent had he been to hear the words.

"I'd been thinking they were being held underground and that confirms it for me. It's not a cold day today, so they weren't at ground level.

"Now. Did anyone else hear that background noise about half-way through Edward talking to the camera?"

This time there was a universal shaking of heads.

"We need to run that through the right equipment to see if we can identify what caused the noise. It was too faint for me to make out.

"I'm also worried that in taking Edward and Daisy, they might be changing a bit. Up to now, it has been clear they were after money, but this feels more staged somehow. I'm not quite sure, but I wonder if they are moving away from simply making money. Could it be that this is no longer enough for these people? If so, what comes next?"

Hooley looked around the room, People were wearing the type of expression he knew he often did himself. They were wondering how Roper had spotted so much that they had missed.

20

Among the many offices brought to a standstill by the illegal broadcast was the headquarters of Britain's brashest morning television station, Wakey Wakey.

The lead presenter was Lancelot Smythe Smythson, a well-fed middle-aged man with the uncanny ability to understand his audience to perfection. What he liked, they liked – and what he hated, they hated. Even his enemies – and they were legion – accepted this made him the most powerful performer on commercial TV. As a result, Smythe-Smythson was never far from controversy. A habit he had got into from a young age when he was expelled from his blue-blooded private school for reasons which remained opaque to this day. He revelled in his reputation, telling his circle of associates. "There is nothing I won't say or do if it gets me an extra viewer."

Now he was looking flushed as he punched the air with joy.

"Only a complete moron wouldn't realise what we're going to be leading on. We could just show that clip of Daisy and get every single viewer in the country tuning in. But that demand for twenty million smackers, it's just what we needed to take this story to the next level." Never scared of hyperbole, he added, "Actually, this isn't going to take it to the next level. It's going to take it to the biggest story, this country and the whole wide world has ever seen."

As he spoke, he was scanning the production office for his sidekick, Tom Brady. The man credited by many for coming up with the story ideas that regularly helped the presenter to scrape the barrel of popular journalism.

"Over here, boss." Brady waved from his position near the water cooler.

Smythe-Smythson gestured for him to come over to his desk. "We need to do something really extraordinary for tomorrow, and I want everyone to know about it in advance. If we play this right, it could get me back in my rightful place on American TV."

In keeping with his typical 'bull in a china shop' approach to life, the presenter didn't notice the expressions that appeared on the faces of his staff as they considered his words. They worked in a cynical world, but this was blatant – the presenter hitching his career to the fortunes of a kidnap victim.

Smythe-Smythson carried on, oblivious to the impact he was having. Even if he had noticed, he wouldn't have cared. He was so thick-skinned he was practically armour-plated.

But Brady was one person he took very seriously, almost as seriously as he took himself. The presenter was intrigued to see that his man was looking exceptionally pleased with himself.

"Come on Brady, you look like a man who's got his hands on the last chocolate biscuit in the tin, so out with it – what's the great plan?"

Brady's grin got even brighter.

"You're going to apologise."

Smythe-Smythson just stared at him, then stared some more before he finally responded. "Have I told you before my family can trace its name back to the Domesday Book?"

"Many times, boss, many times."

"And what is one of the most important things I say that means?"

Brady's grin grew wider. "You say that means you never have to apologise, and you never have to explain."

"So, given that this philosophy has got me where I am today, why on earth are you suggesting that I suddenly change direction?"

His tone sounded cold, but his eyes were bright, betraying his keen interest in getting to the answer.

Brady did not hesitate.

"It's precisely because you've never done it before that it will turbocharge the plan. Everyone knows that you've been a fierce critic of Daisy Daffodil – but now you're truly shocked at what's happening to her, and you realise that, at this time of crisis, everyone needs to get behind Daisy." Brady paused, allowing his plan to sink in. "You have decided to go on Twitter to make the announcement about your apology because you want to make sure as many people as possible recognise the terrible danger she's in. You'll announce that you have personally made a donation to her cause. A very substantial six-figure one, that I will quietly leak to the rest of the media – and you hope that some of your millions of followers can find it in their hearts to send what they can afford to help bring this innocent young woman safely back to her family."

The rest of the crew couldn't decide if this was the most brilliant thing they had heard, or the most cynically calculating.

Smythe-Smythson looked thoughtful. "And when am I going to do all this?"

Brady spread his hands wide.

"Right now. We need to take ownership of this story before anybody else does. We need your name on everyone's lips."

The presenter was now wearing a grin to match that of his sidekick.

"I love it when you come up with something that needs sincerity, Tom. Viewers agree that I am at my very best when I'm being sincere…" He paused. "So, what do you want me to do first?"

21

Misgivings to one side, the Wakey Wakey team, had gone into overdrive to prepare the ground for Smythe-Smythson's announcement. They had been bombarding social media sites all morning, claiming to have an important statement to make on the kidnapping of Daisy Daffodil.

Brian Hooley discovered that the TV station was up to something and asked the Yard's Chief of the Press Bureau to find out what was going on, and if they really had something new. A discrete phone call established it was an editorial promotion linked to Daisy Daffodil, news which disappointed Hooley. He hated Wakey Wakey and its ebullient presenter. He had enjoyed a fantasy where he had arrested all concerned on charges of obstructing a murder inquiry.

The Wakey Wakey editor explained they would be doing a one-off special, a late afternoon slot to set things up for the next day. Which would kick off with a 6am start and a blast of Twitter activity.

"I'm promised it's just showbiz stuff but obviously watch it yourself to double-check," the Press Bureau chief had told Hooley.

Hooley decided to do just that and, with five minutes to go before the special afternoon broadcast, he and Roper decided to go and watch the show with the rest of the team, rather than keeping themselves separate in their own office.

Right on time, the terrestrial station announced it was interrupting the schedules for an "important announcement".

A fanfare of trumpets – which the DCI thought was mainly over the top but was at least tuneful – signalled the arrival on-screen of the infamous television presenter.

Smythe-Smythson was dressed in a formal black suit, in what was clearly intended to be a mark of respect. But just made him look, as one of the junior detectives remarked, "like a fat bouncer." The presenter kept his expression solemn as he stared into the camera. Taking a deep breath, he spoke slowly, each word dipped in sweet sincerity.

"I am here today because I need to admit that I have been wrong, wrong about the Passion Island star Daisy Daffodil. As many of you will know, I have been unhesitating in my criticism of Miss Daffodil. Among many other things, I have accused her of being selfish, greedy and not very intelligent." He paused, shaking his head sadly. "I have said that every move she makes and every word she says is calculated to increase her fan base and make her more money. But everything changed earlier today when that video emerged of her being forced to plead for her life and revealing that her kidnappers were demanding an enormous ransom in return for her freedom. At that very moment, I realised I was wrong to attack a young woman who was only seeking to find her way in the world, using the assets life has given her. For me to question her at this moment would be wrong and hurtful. I want to apologise to her and her family. I'm owning up to my mistakes in misjudging Daisy. I allowed myself to get caught up in all the hype, and I should have known better."

Smythe-Smythson stared deep into the camera. He was radiating empathy.

"I am saying this now because there is no time to lose. It is important that the whole country becomes united in our determination to see her brought home. I am also asking my followers to ask themselves: If this was my daughter, my sister, my friend, what would you do to see her safely returned? The answer, I believe, is that we would all do whatever we could. And that is why I am asking everyone to donate whatever they can afford. It doesn't matter if it's one pound or one thousand pounds, so long as you have the money available and send it to save Daisy, then I can ask no more of you."

He paused and placed his hands together in front of his chest, being careful not to obscure his face. "Please join me," he said, "for a short and silent prayer as we seek her return and those of the other victims."

As the camera panned back, viewers could see a single tear running from his left eye. As he faded from view, the screen filled with information about how to make a donation.

As the broadcast came to an end, Hooley was shaking his head in an exaggerated form of dismay.

"Well you have to hand it to that man – he certainly can turn it on. If I didn't know better, I would have thought he meant all that."

Roper went very still. "Are you saying that he was lying?"

"I would certainly say he was being economical with the truth – and that was all carefully scripted to make him look good. He just wants to make himself part of the story, that's what that's all about."

Roper thought about this for a long moment before he spoke. "But what about that tear rolling down his cheek?"

Hooley shrugged. "He's probably got some eye drops for that."

Roper clenched his fists, pressing them against his thighs as a deep frown appeared. There was no need for a body language expert to spot that Hooley's fellow detective was seriously annoyed.

"That is absolutely terrible. It means he's just doing it for his own benefit, and to improve viewing figures on his show. We should be able to arrest him for that, it's quite awful."

Usually, Hooley would have jokingly agreed with him before steering the conversation elsewhere – but he could tell this had really got under Roper's skin. He was going to have tackle this head-on or risk Roper going off on a tangent.

"Put it out of your mind, Jonathan. It really is just the way things are. He's hardly the first person to pretend to be someone they're not and say things to make people like him." He paused. "I do like your idea about arresting him for telling lies – but, if we went down that path, all the prisons would be full of politicians in no time."

He glanced at Roper to see if that had got through and was relieved to see that he looked calm enough. The trick now was to get him thinking about the investigation. He went for the question which had been on his mind since this morning.

"When are you going to share your thoughts about what's going on here? You said, and not for the first time that things were going to change."

In response, Roper went deep into thought. A lot of people thought his ability to instantly switch from anger to analysis unsettling. In this instance, Hooley was glad of it. He left Roper to marshal his thoughts and was rewarded after just a few minutes. The younger man folded his arms, looked down at his feet and then back up at his boss.

"I think I am beginning to see what is going on. I think we might see a significant escalation."

22

Ricky Horton was just twenty-two years old, six-feet, five inches tall – with dyed blonde hair, a mega-watt smile and blessed with great genes that allowed him to boast a remarkable eight-pack. He was the envy of most men. The combination made him the star of the Passion Island rival, "Sun, Sea and Love". And when it came to celebrity power, he was Daisy Daffodil's direct rival, boasting a little under twenty-two million followers on Instagram.

Right now, he was enjoying what was, for him, a hearty breakfast of a glass of water and half an apple. Ricky may not have been the smartest man in the world. Still he understood that he owed everything he had achieved to his good looks and extraordinary physique. Consequently, he was meticulous about what he put into his body.

In the Foyer and Reading Room at Claridges Hotel, Ricky sat opposite his agent, Johnny Sturgess, who was showing no such restraint as he tucked into the hotel's famous Full English. Sturgess was in his mid-forties, wearing a striped business shirt paired with jeans, a combination that did nothing to make him look more youthful even though he thought it did.

"This is one of the best sausages I've had in years," he said, taking a huge bite of a perfectly browned chipolata before enthusiastically spearing something that made Horton's eight pack ripple in rebellion.

"Look at this," he said, waving it in front of Horton "This is delicious. I'm not normally a fan of black pudding, but this one is excellent. There's a nice spicy kick to it."

The pudding disappeared into his mouth to be chewed with enthusiasm.

Horton was not known for his conversation skills and merely shrugged. As far as he was concerned, food was an enemy to be defeated at every opportunity. When he wasn't filming the show that had made him famous, he spent most of his time in Ibiza, working out and topping up his tan while living on a diet of raw vegetables and small amounts of fresh fruit.

It had taken an astonishingly good offer to get him back to the UK. Two weeks previously, his agent had been approached by a middleman for a US TV company who wanted to use Horton as one of the principal characters in a documentary series about the power of celebrity. The company was insisting on rigid confidentiality, so no Instagram posts or hints on other social media platforms. In return for this "radio silence", they were paying generous expenses – hence the upmarket hotel – and there was the promise of a two-hundred thousand pound signing-on fee, with an eye-watering one million pound bonus if the show went into production.

The agent did briefly wrestle with his conscience as he wondered if it was too good to be true. Still, the company seemed to check out, and the thought of his twenty per cent cut quickly drowned out his misgivings.

Finishing his breakfast, he poured himself another cup of tea before leaning back with a satisfied expression on his face.

"I've just had a text message to confirm the production team's limo is on the way. They should be with us in about ten minutes. Are you still OK about going on your own?"

A close friend of the agent had been taken ill the previous afternoon and had been rushed to the Chelsea and Westminster Hospital. Sturgess was due there in an hour to get updated on his condition. He intended to catch up with his client later in the day.

Horton nodded.

"As soon as you're in the car, I'll be off to the hospital. I'll let you know if there's going to be a change of plan but, otherwise, expect me later. The only thing I would say to you is, please don't worry if they start trying to get you to sign anything else. Just tell them you want to wait until I get there. That's all they need to know."

The pair finished up and made their way into the lobby, only to discover the driver was already asking for them at reception. Under the close supervision of the uniformed doorman, he led them outside to a stretched, customised, Mercedes saloon, into which Horton clambered, settling back against the black leather seats. He might not say much, but Ricky Horton appreciated luxury and sighed contentedly as the car pulled into the traffic. Totally ignoring his agent who was waving goodbye.

He didn't notice when the driver locked the rear doors, although he did wonder at the thick piece of glass that slid silently into place between the rear cabin and the front. He finally spoke when the windows, already quite dark, became impossible to see through.

"Is everything OK? I can't really see out of the windows."

"Nothing to worry about, sir," came the driver's voice through a microphone. "We just want to keep you safe from prying eyes."

As he spoke, the partition glass also went black, leaving Horton completely cut off from the outside world. He began to wonder if he should be worried. He tried his mobile but couldn't get a signal.

Fifteen minutes later, he was disoriented, out of his depth and had no idea what was happening.

It was dawning on him that he might have a problem and became aware of a sensation that rarely crossed his path… fear!

23

After watching the two detectives leave, Peter Webb had picked up his landline. If he didn't make the call to his boss immediately, he was worried he would lose his nerve. It wasn't every day you had to ask your employer to lend you one million pounds, in cash.

He called Gerald Stone on his direct line and was pleased when the senior partner not only answered but was full of sympathy. He told Webb he would discuss it with the other partners and get back to him as soon as possible. He understood the urgency.

Less than an hour later, Stone was back on the phone.

His opening remarks could not have sounded more reassuring.

"Let me assure you, Peter, that we are all more than aware of the terrible pressure you and your wife are under. Please tell Liz that my wife sends her love and prayers in the hope this can be resolved as quickly as possible." He took a breath. "Everyone wants to find the right solution for you, but clearly the amount of money being discussed is huge, so we need to think very carefully about how we go about this. Would it be possible for me to come and visit you at your home? I know we need to do this quickly, so I'm suggesting that I leave now. I can be with you inside half an hour."

Webb agreed to the meeting and ended the call with a sense of foreboding. His boss seemed to be making the right sort of noises, but there was something else there, something that didn't strike the right note – he would find out soon enough.

Twenty-five minutes later, one of the policemen guarding the house announced that a "Gerald Stone" was on the doorstep and asking to come in. Webb went to meet him and took Stone down to the kitchen. While his boss sat at the kitchen table gazing out at the small garden, Webb busied himself making tea, seeking comfort in an ingrained habit that was almost a ritual. Boil fresh water, let it cool ever so slightly, pour it on the tea bag and leave for three minutes.

He placed the cups on the table and sat opposite. The silence built, the pair ignoring each other in the way people do when they have something important and personal to discuss. It was Stone who made the first attempt at starting the conversation. Webb couldn't help but note his forehead was shiny with the faintest sheen of sweat. He hoped that was down to it being a warm day and the stressful situation, not because he was about to deliver bad news.

"I want to start by telling you again how much everyone in the office is right behind you. I've got the HR people involved to make sure that we do everything possible and I've commissioned legal advice to ensure that whatever we do it's completely above board and can't come back and have implications for you."

Webb blinked rapidly. "Implications?" he asked. "I don't understand what implications are you talking about?"

Stone coloured slightly. "Much as we would all like to wave a magic wand, there are important considerations that we need to take into account. We have to protect your best interests, and ours as well."

Up to this point, Webb had felt almost dizzy with the tiredness. But now, as Stone spoke, a kind of cold fury was focusing his mind.

At a primal level, Stone was aware that the other man was changing, becoming more threatening. It triggered his "fight or flight" response, increasing his blood pressure and releasing adrenaline which led to him easing his chair away as if preparing to flee.

Webb was holding his emotions in check through sheer willpower. He spoke through gritted teeth, his voice barely rising above a whisper, every word spat out.

"I don't have time for these stupid games. My wife doesn't have time, and my son most certainly doesn't have time. He's fighting for his life, and I will do anything to help him." He slammed his hand on the table to emphasise the point, making his boss jump to his feet in fright.

Stone held out his hands in a warding gesture. "Please, don't shoot the messenger."

Webb didn't reply, just stared ahead, his eyes blazing and looking, Stone thought, like a man who was no longer entirely sane.

"We took professional advice like we always do," Stone stammered, desperate to be out of here. "You know that better than most people. If we don't follow legal advice, then what's the point?"

Stone thought this was a point well-made – but then he saw that Webb had clenched his fists. For the first time, he noticed that his colleague was a much bigger man than he was.

He hurried on, trying to hide his sudden fear. "What I'm about to say is going to disappoint you, and I wish it wasn't so, but it is what it is. The lawyers say that, if we gave you company money, we would be in breach of our own rules, ones designed to stop partners helping themselves to cash. We could face a legal challenge and even risk imprisonment." He was in the finishing strait now and rushed on, desperate to get the words out and get out of there. "Obviously this is bad news for you and all the partners were gutted when they were told. There was a unanimous vote to see if we could help on a personal level. But I'm afraid that's not going to be possible either. Despite our dearest wish to help, we've been advised that handing over personal money would open up all sorts of tax implications, both now and in the future. It would mean that any money we gave you would be liable for unspecified tax amounts for you and us."

He paused and glanced anxiously at Webb, who had gone a disturbingly dark colour. He waited to see if Webb wanted to speak, but the man remained silent, his fierce expression unwavering.

"We put our heads together and managed to come up with something that might help. There's an Australian bank that specialises in more risky loans. I've spoken to them, and they are willing to take your case on. I'm afraid I was presumptuous enough to ask them to come directly to you here at your home." Stone glanced at his watch. "I'm expecting their chief negotiator any moment now. Let me go and see if he's outside and I will bring him in. Assuming that is okay with you?"

After that, Stone all but ran from the kitchen and up the stairs. Dashing out of the front door, he was relieved to find a well-dressed man, in his 30s, waiting at the foot of the steps.

"Mr Brian Preston from Sydney Bank?"

The man nodded and smiled. A few minutes later, Stone had left him in the kitchen, and was grateful to be able to escape.

Webb looked at this new arrival and sighed. His rage was still burning, but he was no fool. He understood what was happening here and that this man probably represented his only hope of raising the cash.

He took a deep breath.

"Tell me how this works?"

Taylor smiled at him.

"I understand this is pretty rough for you, but I am strictly business. There is nothing personal here. I am putting an initial value of six million pounds on this house. It may be more than that, but that figure gives us something to work from, and the percentages remain the same whether you sell it for six million pounds or seven million pounds. Even ten million pounds. What's important to you is that if you were to sign up now, the money would be sitting in your account within 24 hours from now, maybe even a little sooner."

Webb knew enough about money to recognize there was a "but" coming. "Go on. Talk me through the deal."

"Given your circumstances, I have been authorized to offer you the most favourable terms. We agree on a minimum price for your home, as I just mentioned, and you pay us an agreed percentage of the amount you receive.

"On the assumption, you get six million pounds for the property, that will see us split the proceeds fifty/fifty, minus the million loan. You also get the one million pounds you need by this time tomorrow. We can do that in cash."

He sat back in his chair, folding his arms. "I know you won't find any lender willing to do this so fast and with such good terms."

Webb tried to make sense of what was happening. His boss had turned his back, so this man was going to take his house, something he would do to save his son.

"I have a couple of questions," he said. "When will the house be placed on the market, and what happens if we sell it for more than the agreed price?"

Taylor replied, "Normally we would put the property on the market straight away – but in recognition of your circumstances, we would leave it for six months. Regarding the other question, we would keep twenty per cent of the additional money. I think we can both agree that the six million pound asking price is the least we can expect. But if it's lower, we still get back the million and split the difference. I'm a father myself, and I want to do the best for you as I can."

The banker paused and extended his hand. "So, what do you think… do we have a deal?"

24

The warning surfaced from the Dark Web. It was terse and to the point.

"Contestant update at 4:30 PM, GMT."

Hooley seized the opportunity to press Roper again about what he meant by a competitive element about to be introduced. But Roper was keeping his thoughts tight.

"I don't want to make any guesses, not when it is almost certain we are only a few hours away from finding out if I am right."

Hooley swallowed his frustration. Even though he was desperate to keep the momentum rolling along, he knew there was no way he could persuade Roper to speak out. Roper had always been this way; once he'd set his lines in the sand, he could not be shifted. The expression 'stubborn as a mule' barely covered it. If Roper said a thing, he meant it.

The DCI was equally unsuccessful in persuading him to watch the Golden Shot update in the main incident room, the younger man adamant he needed to watch while sitting at his own desk.

Hooley sighed. Joining the rest of the team was good for morale since it gave people a chance to see Roper in action while he could hide behind the activity. Knowing there was nothing to be gained by having a discussion, he determined that he would spend some time with the team later this afternoon. When you were running major investigations, it was easy to forget all the tiny little details that needed checking or following up.

Decision made Hooley put it out of his mind as he tried not to spend the next couple of hours clock-watching.

He was also regretting eating two blueberry muffins at lunchtime. That was one of the pitfalls that came from sitting near Roper. The man could eat a mountain of food and never gain an ounce in weight. It had been Roper's turn to get lunch today, and he had arrived back with a bulging bag of goodies from which the DCI had happily helped himself… with a little too much relish.

Finally, the Contestant Update arrived. Roper called up the site on his monitor, and the pair settled down to watch. It was then that Roper came out with one of his unique insights.

"They're going to announce that they've grabbed someone else. If I have worked this out, it's going to be another celebrity like Daisy Daffodil."

The DCI stared at him in amazement but, before he could respond, the intro to the Golden Shot started up. Moments later, a confused looking Ricky Horton was staring out of the screen. He began speaking hesitantly, apparently from an autocue.

"The Golden Shot has realised there is a big difference between having friends on Instagram and actually having friends. Despite having millions of apparently dedicated followers, very few of them seem willing to part with any money to save Daisy. Some people are even refusing to send money because they say this is all a publicity stunt to make Daisy rich."

Ricky's face creased as he turned to the left, apparently listening to someone. Then he turned back to the camera, squinted and started reading again.

"The producers could waste time telling you that Daisy's life is hanging by a thread, but it is clear people have made their minds up. So, here is something to make you all think again. We're going to find out who is really the most popular: Daisy or Ricky?" He jabbed his finger at his chest.

"And you get the chance to put your money where your mouth is. From tomorrow, both accounts will be set to zero and the first one to get to £20 million wins. Simple as that. Winner takes all and will be dropped off, safe and sound, at a location of our choosing. The loser gets to play the Golden Shot." Ricky paused as if unable to complete his sentence. Finally, he uttered, "They will not be so lucky."

The image changed to the man in the clown face. Before he could finish his "A Show To Die For" catchphrase, Roper shut him off.

"How did you work out that was going to happen?" Hooley asked.

Roper leaned back in his chair. "The amount of money they were asking for was never going to happen, so they were either being stupid, or they had something else in mind. We know they are far from stupid – so what were they really up to? That's when I started thinking about the way social media works. We know it's not about getting to the truth. It's about saying things that enough people will respond to. It doesn't matter whether you think it's true or not. Those ideas, with one side, pitched against another, are the way online life works, so I thought it was certain that they would come up with a competition. One person against another – nothing in between."

Hooley was momentarily lost for words. There was something about the way he saw the world that allowed Roper to come up with such insights.

"When you explain it, it all makes perfect sense. But can I ask… You were very angry with the way the Wakey Wakey team were making things up as they went along. Yet with this, you seem quite calm…"

"I asked myself the same thing actually. I think it is because I make a difference between the internet and people."

Before Hooley had a chance to contemplate this, his phone rang. Seeing it was building security, he took it. As he listened, a frown appeared.

"Please don't think I'm doubting you, or telling you how to do your job," he began, "but are you sure it's him and not some idiot reporter thinking he's going to make a name for himself? I presume you've checked his ID?"

There was a brief pause, and Hooley took the chance to mouth, "Building security say they've got Peter Webb, apparently down there. He's asking to see us, but I've asked them to check."

Roper started tapping at his keyboard then swung his monitor around so that Hooley could see. The camera system was brand new and gave them a crystal-clear view of the entrance.

"It's Peter Webb, alright," said the DCI. "what on earth has got him out of the house."

Roper did some more tapping and added sound. They heard Webb say. "I've got my driving license in my wallet it's got my photo on it. Will that do?"

The desk sergeant nodded. "That will do fine, Sir. Just take it nice and slowly please."

Webb handed over the small plastic card. The man studied it carefully before showing it to a female colleague. The woman also studied it carefully before nodding.

"Thank you, Sir. I just need you to pass through the security scanners, and then DCI Hooley will be here shortly." He pointed at a plastic tray. All metal objects in there please."

Webb emptied his pockets and stepped through the airport-style scanner. The alarm went off.

“You must have forgotten something, said the woman.”

Hooley watched a look of realization cross Webb’s face. He reached behind him.

“I forgot this. I don’t know how. It’s why I’m here.”

With that, he produced a gun.

Hooley gasped as time seemed to slow down. What happened next seemed in slow motion. The woman shouted “gun” before stepping forward and removing it from his hand. At the same time, the male guard stepped in and put him flat on the ground. The woman helped pull Webb’s hands behind his back and handcuff him.

The watching Hooley felt like giving them a round of applause. The pair had been brilliant, and no one was injured. He and Roper raced out of the office to run downstairs.

By the time they got there, the entranceway was full of armed police with a contrite looking Webb at the centre of attention.

The DCI walked over to him.

“I hope you’ve got an explanation for this. And it had better be good.”

25

The gun turned out to be an air gun and, even better, close study of the surveillance video made it clear that Webb was attempting to extract it from behind his back to show it to the security team.

It also emerged that he had ended up taking drastic action after his firm had turned down his plea for help and had come to Victoria to hand himself into Brian Hooley.

He was being held in one of the interview rooms, and after studying him through the two-way glass, Hooley decided to talk to him.

Webb looked up as the detective appeared in the doorway, Hooley took a seat facing the man and said. "No-one is more aware of your personal circumstances than me, but what you did was incredibly stupid. You should thank everything you hold sacred that this didn't turn out far worse."

Hooley took a deep breath. "I'm not going to say you're a lucky man because your current situation makes you far from lucky. But I think it's reasonable to say that you have been very fortunate."

Hooley thought Webb looked tired but was otherwise well, apart from the livid red mark on his forehead, sustained when he was forcibly disarmed.

The DCI judged he was in a fit state to be released... Once he'd had a bit longer in his cell.

An hour passed and the DCI felt happy to let Webb go once they had another quick chat. He walked back into the interview room and said. "I'll start with the good news, which is that Mr Stone received superficial injuries as the pellet from your air gun did not make it through the material of his trousers. You did give him a very nasty fright, however – and, for all you know, you could have induced a heart attack. Despite this, Mr Stone is adamant that he has no wish to press charges."

He paused again to study Webb; this was an important decision and he wasn't going to rush at it. Then, raising an eyebrow, he went on, "To be honest, I don't think he had much choice. It was pointed out to him that his actions towards you were less than charitable. It was further pointed out that, if news got out and appeared on social media, he would probably become the most hated man in London – and would probably need to be taken into custody for his own safety."

The DCI was pleased to see this brought a faint smile. It showed that, somewhere deep inside, Webb was holding on to a shred of humour.

"I've spent some time on the phone with my boss, the Commissioner, because you have, even allowing for your personal circumstances, committed some very serious offences. Mr Webb, not only could you have hurt Mr Stone – arriving here with a weapon was very foolish. We have armed security here. You're extremely fortunate that their training is so good – otherwise, you might have been shot."

Hooley paused. Making this decision was obviously giving him real heartache. "So, even though Mr Stone is willing to forgo charging you, we – that is, the police – need to decide what to do with you."

Hooley offered Mr Webb a look. "Perhaps this might be a good time for you to offer your thoughts?"

Webb looked up, making eye contact before shaking his head slowly.

"I'm not a violent man, Detective Chief Inspector. But the cruel way Stone refused to help me get the money together to rescue my son filled me with rage. All that talk of tax liabilities and deeds of association forbidding the company giving me a loan – it was just lies. To make it worse, he sent in someone who wanted to steal my house from me."

Webb finally fixed Hooley with a look. "Don't get me wrong. I'll pay any amount to get Edward back, including selling the house, but it felt like, at the moment of my greatest need, I was being thrown to the dogs. Twenty-six years I've worked there. I've always been loyal and hardworking, yet this is how they treat me."

Hooley was giving him a look of the deepest sympathy. "You might be surprised at how many people share that view, Mr Webb. And I may have some good news on that front. Mr Stone would like you to know that he is willing to take fresh legal advice. He is now acutely aware that his current position might end up damaging his business profile. So it is in everyone's interest that he finds a way to help you. You will, of course, have to use your house as collateral, but I understand the terms will be more amenable."

Webb looked like a drowning man who has been thrown a lifeline, the deep worry lines around his eyes visibly improving.

"That is a good outcome," the DCI continued, "so now we just need to decide what to do about your arriving here with a weapon."

"And?" asked Webb. He looked hopeful.

"And… the Commissioner accepts your case that you came here to turn yourself in because you wanted to talk to myself and Jonathan Roper," Hooley began.

"She feels there is no public interest to be gained by charging you – at this stage. And she has given me the discretion to decide if you can be released on extended police bail. To do that, Mr Webb, I'll need your word you won't engage in any more ill-thought-out vigilante attacks. You must also promise not to try and leave your home unless accompanied by a police officer."

Hooley hardened his voice now, though Webb seemed to understand. "I don't want to labour the point, Mr Webb, but you and your wife have got to stick together to get through this. Having you languishing in a cell is not going to help. So... can I let you go? And do you promise that the next time you get an idea like this into your head, you count to ten – and then, if you still feel like doing a Rambo impersonation, you call me instead?"

Webb stood up and nodded solemnly at the policeman.

Hooley grinned and held out his hand. "Good. Then I'll have you home very soon – I just want our doctor to give you a once-over before you go. He's in the building, so he won't be long. I've got your phone here so you can call your wife, let her know you'll be back very soon."

Hooley was turning to leave when, suddenly, the door opened, and Roper marched in.

There he stopped dead, ignoring Hooley completely, and stared directly at Webb.

"Mr Webb, the Golden Shot people know you are here."

26

The news took Hooley entirely by surprise, and the more he thought about the implications, the less he liked it. Was it a mole? Or had the Golden Shot brigade accessed the building's security cameras so that they could see what was going on? Either answer was bad news.

Webb was stunned, most probably thinking that the kidnappers had found a way of keeping him under constant surveillance. A bout of paranoia was the last thing Hooley needed.

Roper snapped him out of his reverie.

"I think we need to show Mr Webb, the latest video."

The DCI was about to offer a platitude when Roper proved he was experiencing one of his rare moments of empathy and offered Webb a measure of reassurance.

"I hate to ask you, but maybe there will be some clue that you spot that we would never pick up. Keep in mind that they want you thinking they can always see you, which is nonsense, especially since we debugged your home."

Roper didn't wait for a reply, he simply headed out of the cell and back towards the staircase. The DCI gestured Webb to go next, and Hooley himself made up the rear of the short column which climbed back to their office.

Once they had reached the office, Roper went straight to his desk and launched his specialist browser to access the Dark Web. Quickly, he found the message set up by the Golden Shot team.

He was about to click on it when he did a double-take.

"I think they've updated the message. This one is much bigger. The last one just showed a still picture of Edward and had a voice-over. I think this one may include a video clip."

He kept looking at his screen until an impatient Hooley urged him onward. "Get on with it, Jonathan. You can check out the details after we find out what they have to say."

Roper scowled, but his own interest was sharp enough to encourage him to call it up.

Webb and the DCI stood flanking him as he tapped at his keyboard and watched the monitor flicker into life. At first, the screen was empty; then the video began with a black cab pulling up at a stretch of pavement. After a few moments, Peter Webb could be seen getting out, looking around and then walking off to the right of the shot. The picture panned round to capture him pushing his way through a double door. The picture quality was sharp and seemed professional.

"That's this building, here," Webb realised, "and that was me just a few hours ago. How did they do that?"

Roper answered. "They must have tracked you here. I need to check the external cameras to see if we can pick them up when they got here."

Hooley was making for the door. "I can't believe they are still around, but I need to check. Be back in a minute. Stay where you are Mr Webb. I'll be back by the time Jonathan has the security footage called up."

Roper was able to use the time to find a pair of support workers to work the video files. They were set to go by the time Hooley returned. As he'd anticipated, the gang was long gone.

All three watched as one of the tech's connected to footage from a pair of cameras guarding the front entrance.

An expectant hush fell over the room as the film moved backwards at a rapid pace.

The video looked like a blur to Hooley, but he knew more efficient eyes would spot when they were at the right spot. Sure enough, it was a young woman tech who reacted first.

"There – stop it there!"

Now the video played at normal speed, the clip showing a white van pulling up at the pavement. A few seconds later, the passenger door opened and a man carrying a TV-style video camera clambered out, leaving his door open and partially blocking the pavement.

He moved to the centre of the pavement, all the time pointing his camera back towards the station entrance before he calmly walked back to the unmarked van and took off.

"Could anyone see anything that would identify him or the van?"

The sharp-eyed woman spoke again. "He was almost using that camera as a shield to hide his face. Even the van's number plates were obscured." She hesitated before going on. "There's a second camera by the door. Maybe that was looking straight at him?"

"Well done," said the DCI, then directed his gaze to the tech who was operating the access to the feeds. "Can you find it as quickly as you can?"

A few seconds later, they were once again staring at a high-speed rewind until they reached the right moment. Now the atmosphere in the room was electric in anticipation.

A new angle showed the van pulling up. There was a collective groan as they saw that the number plate was obscured, then fresh groans as the cameraman got out with his face still blocked by his gear. These quickly turned to cheers as the man tracked around to his right, bringing half his face into view.

It wasn't perfect, but it was the first real break any investigation team had achieved. All around the investigation room, high-fives were being exchanged.

Even the ordinarily dour DCI was grinning – but, when he spotted that Roper was looking deeply worried, he soon stopped. Quickly, he closed the gap between them.

"What is it? What's wrong?"

Roper looked up his eyes alight. "How did they get that film of Mr Webb? There's no way they could have been waiting there – they would have been moved on – so they must have followed him." Roper shook his head. "He told us that after he shot Stone at the office in Shepherd's Bush that he just ran out of the building and got a cab to bring him here. So that means… They must have been waiting outside the office. They must have seen him go in and come out. I did think about them picking him up at his home, but they would have been spotted down there, especially with so many people crowding around. No," said Roper, "they got him at his office, I'm sure. But my question is – what were they doing there? They can't have been hanging around waiting for Webb."

Hooley thought about it, then felt his blood run cold.

"They're going back in there to get someone else."

27

The response car was waiting for them as they raced out of the building. The moment the rear doors slammed shut, the driver took off into the traffic.

Hooley resisted the urge to call his duty inspector. He'd already spoken to the man and was confident that every action was being put in place. He'd slow things down if he tried to intervene.

Traffic was amazingly light, and in no time at all, they were racing past Hyde Park, heading east. The first real bottleneck came at the junction of Kensington High Street and Church Street, which the driver dealt with by racing through the lights on the wrong side of the road.

Hooley managed to keep his eyes open long enough to acknowledge the man had taken a reasonable risk before he involuntarily shut them tight. For a time, as they hurtled eastward, he kept them closed. Then, a call over the car radio made his eyes snap open.

"Emergency at Stone and Partners, Shepherd's Bush. Ambulance requested."

As Hooley and Roper digested the implications, a more urgent voice came through.

"Reports of officers down. I repeat. Officers down at Stone and Partners, Shepherd's Bush."

The response was almost instantaneous.

"Armed response unit ninety seconds out."

"Paramedic two minutes out."

There followed a few seconds of silence before control relayed a fresh update.

"Eyewitness reports an exchange of shots between officers and suspects."

Another brief pause.

"Urgent update. An officer at the scene confirms two officers down and two suspects down."

"Armed response unit on scene."

Another short gap.

"Paramedic approaching scene."

"Paramedic, given the go-ahead to approach."

A fresh voice.

"This is PC Norman Mann. Suspects have departed the scene. Officers are down on the pavement outside the building. They are not responding to resuscitation attempts. Armed response officers are securing the scene. Paramedic is still working on officers."

The PC was speaking slowly and calmly, his steady voice contrasting with the vivid picture his words were painting.

A furious Hooley slammed his fist into his knee.

"I should have anticipated something like this could happen. This is going to be on my conscience." He looked at the driver.

"Three minutes sir, we might even be there faster."

The DCI stared out of the back window. They weren't that far away, yet out there, everything looked normal. No hints of the bloodbath that had just played out.

As they closed in on the scene, they slowed down to allow two ambulances through. Two marked police cars were present, and the wail of sirens announced the imminent arrival of more emergency response units.

The driver got them within fifty yards; then Hooley and Roper were out and running. As they got closer, the two men could see confirmation of what they had been listening to.

Two hooded suspects were lying on the ground. They had suffered severe chest wounds and were lying inert. Handguns, which the DCI assumed belonged to the bad guys, were clearly visible on the ground.

About twenty feet away, two police officers were also lying motionless on the pavement. Despite their wounds, paramedics were working hard on them – but it was a lost cause. Their Heckler and Koch carbines lay on the pavement next to the bodies.

Taking in the position of the bodies, Hooley estimated that the suspects had approached the accountancy firm and been challenged by the two officers, who'd given a good account of themselves. It was cold comfort that no civilians had been caught up in the exchange.

Hooley swallowed hard as bile burned the back of his throat. He was close enough to see that neither of the dead officers was much older than mid-20s. He wondered what family had been left behind: parents, brothers, sisters, wives, children… It was painful to think about.

His thoughts had kicked into overdrive by seeing these bodies but thinking about the devastation of friends and relatives soon sobered him up. The least he could do for the two dead men was make sure he ran the best possible investigation. That started now.

Hooley looked around. At the edges of the police cordon, a crowd of spectators had built. While some were crying, others had arrived simply to gawk. Photographs were being taken. Whatever the motivation of these spectators, they needed to be kept as far away from the crime scene as possible.

Looking around, he noticed two police constables and called them over.

"I want this scene as tight as possible, so keep those people pushed back. About fifty feet should do it."

One of the men turned straight away to carry out his order, but the other held back and nodded at Hooley.

"PC Mann, sir. I was first responder. This is my patch. I have some information that may help."

Hooley nodded, inviting the constable to elaborate.

"As I approached the scene, I heard six loud bangs, which I thought were gunshots. I started running and got here just as two men jumped into a van parked on the opposite side of the street. It was too far away for me to see much, but it was a Ford Transit. It was white, not very clean and I can't be sure about the number plate, but I think it started with HJ."

Hooley felt a surge of hope. It wasn't a breakthrough, but even a partial number helped. PC Mann's account confirmed that the armed officers had been outgunned.

"How confident are you about that HJ?"

"Pretty confident, sir. I've got excellent eyesight, and it was only because the vehicle was moving away, that I didn't get the full number."

The DCI patted the man on the shoulder as he punched in the speed dial for the duty inspector, quickly passing on the information so that it could be distributed throughout the Met.

Roper chipped in. Like the DCI, he was jumping on anything positive.

"That could be vital. Even if we don't find them now, we have something to work with for an in-depth CCTV search." He nodded, making a mental assessment. "Susan Brooker should be back in London today or tomorrow, so she can try out the new algorithm. She says it's amazingly fast. It will be fantastic to see it in action."

Hooley was delighted at the news. They were going to need maximum firepower – brains as well as brawn – to bring down these people. Having Brooker on board could only help.

Gathering himself, Hooley thanked PC Mann again, then started walking towards the entrance to the accountancy firm. As he stepped inside, Roper on his heels, he saw that the immediate area was devoid of people. Staff on the upstairs floors had locked themselves into their offices, not yet willing to trust the area was clear.

At the far end of the reception area, a uniformed officer was standing in front of a door. He gathered himself as Hooley walked over, maintaining his station in front of what Hooley could now see was the entrance to the ladies' lavatory.

Hooley stepped up, raised an eyebrow and said, "Am I right in thinking you have someone in there, constable?"

"Yes, sir. I'm PC Harry Davey, and there's a young woman in there. She's very shaken, but I've had a brief word with her, and she saw something of what happened.

I took the view that I should make sure she remained safe and was available to be spoken to."

Hooley smiled his approval. "That's smart work, PC Davey. What sort of state is our witness in? She's just been through a remarkable ordeal..."

As he finished speaking, the door opened to reveal a small, neat woman who had been crying. Flapping her hand at her eyes, she said, "Don't worry about these. It was a terrible shock, but I want to do what I can. If I can help you get who did this, I'm your woman."

Hooley smiled at her bravery. "Thank you. I'm DCI Brian Hooley, and this is Jonathan Roper. Would you mind telling us what your name is?"

"It's Sally, Sally Taylor, Detective Chief Inspector. My dad was in the force, so I kind of know what to expect."

"OK, Miss Taylor. If you could take us through it, from the beginning, that would be perfect."

She produced a quick smile and puffed her cheeks. "Could you give me a minute to clean up, blow my nose and just tidy up a little bit? I feel a fright."

She went back into the ladies and Hooley could hear water running as she cleaned up. A few minutes later, she was back, looking a little more human. Hooley noticed that she had the same sort of blue eyes as his daughter.

He smiled encouragingly at her, and she launched in. To his joy, she was the sort of witness who had a clear recall and the temperament to describe it in detail. A lot of witnesses could be very random in their approach. You got there in the end, but there was always confusion along the way.

"I'm just a temp here, and this was my second day on the job. I knew what had happened here before, but I thought that, with the police actually on guard… well, my dad says it would have been amazing for them to come back with the Old Bill in place."

Hooley nodded in agreement. In any other case, her dad would have been right. It was ringing alarm bells that they had been so willing to take on an armed response team. The officers had been patrolling with weapons on display so they could not have been missed.

She carried on. "This isn't the busiest place, to be honest, and I know this is going to sound like one of those 'careful what you wish for' moments, but I was a bit bored. I was seriously thinking about phoning my office and asking for something different when I got all the excitement I could handle. I heard a car, or van maybe – I didn't see it – screech to a halt outside and then all hell broke loose. I've never heard machine-gun fire before, but I did then. I was terrified, frozen where I was standing and looking out of the window."

She steeled herself before she went on. "Two police officers came running towards the front entrance. They were firing, and I could hear screams. I guessed people were getting hit. Then there was more gunfire, and the two policemen fell to the ground. I could see blood on the pavement."

Choking back a sob she carried on. "Those poor men. They were so brave. One of them was on the door when I arrived and gave me a lovely smile. I remember thinking he was quite hot..."

Hooley thought she might stop again, but she was determined to get her story told.

"I was still behind the reception desk when the lift pinged, and the doors opened. I saw Mr Stone – but, before I could say anything, he stepped out, just as two men wearing balaclavas ran inside the building. They saw Mr Stone and grabbed him, virtually frog-marching him outside. I heard the vehicle start-up, and that was it, they were gone." She shook her head in mute disbelief. "At the time, it felt like it was going on for hours, but I doubt if the whole thing lasted more than sixty seconds – a bit like that film title 'Gone in Sixty Seconds'."

Hooley had never seen the film in question, but he recognised when things were playing out to a script, with the bad guys pulling the strings. If it hadn't been for Roper's insights, they wouldn't even have managed to get this close. He blinked. Ten minutes earlier, and they'd have been in the middle of a gun battle.

"Just to double-check – you're quite sure it was Mr Stone they grabbed?"

"Yes. Quite sure. The HR lady was adamant that she show me who he was. She said she didn't want the boss getting hassled on his way in and out."

Hooley got on his phone. He had an update for the duty inspector. They would also need to check out the HR lady. Maybe she was very efficient – but maybe, just maybe, she had some hidden agenda.

28

The killing of the two officers had alerted the media and the online media, and in the absence of facts, were asking difficult questions. A tricky case was getting worse.

On the ride back to Victoria, Hooley had been hoping that Roper would offer some insights. But the younger man was totally silent, lost in his own thoughts. Even when they returned to their own office, Roper simply stared into space for five minutes, then announced he was going for lunch. Before Hooley could react, he was out of the door and promising to return shortly.

The DCI watched him go, aware that this might be considered an odd time to be fixating on sandwiches. It felt like the case was going backwards, and they needed to be working harder to get a result.

But he didn't have such an ego that he recognised he needed Roper at his intuitive best to get that break. And the best way of achieving that was allowing Roper to go on a food run. A hungry Roper was a distracted Roper. He also suspected, in defiance of the scientific evidence, that the faster Roper's brain turned, the more calories he burned through.

A short while later, a pile of sandwiches was dumped in front of him – all of them, to his dismay, containing egg in one form or another.

To cap it all, he had the strongest instinct that he was going to receive a lecture, whether he wanted one or not.

Letting out a gentle sigh, he poked the packets in front of him. He was about to be proved right.

The moment Roper started speaking, Hooley braced. He recognised the tone of voice instantly. It was the one that would brook no interference, a voice used by precocious young children explaining how technology works to an especially slow adult.

Roper was off. "I've majored on egg sandwiches because I think you could do with a boost of Omega oils. This case is getting quite complicated, even for me, and I am not sure you are thinking hard enough."

Hooley narrowed his eyes. He was thinking very hard at the moment, imagining what one of the egg sandwiches would look like if he squashed it on Roper's head. Tempted as he was, he resisted the urge.

Roper was blithely unaware of how close he was to sporting a new look in food fashion.

"At one point this morning, I noticed you were breathing through your mouth. This is not a good look and something you do when you are intellectually overloaded."

"Intellectually overloaded?" Hooley was so outraged the words came out slowly and awkwardly.

Roper seized his moment. "You see. You are even talking strangely – as though you have some sort of brain impediment. I don't think we can rule out a tumour, but I think it is because you are finding this hard."

Hooley was so enraged he lost the power of speech altogether. Going extremely red, he issued a series of squeaks and grunts as he attempted to fight back.

Roper studied him carefully.

"You really do need to calm down. Going as red as that cannot be good for you. Why can't you talk? Are you having a stroke? Is that it? Shall I call an ambulance?"

By now, Hooley was starting to wonder if he had wandered into a parallel universe. Issuing a strangled cry,

he waved Roper away and headed for the toilets. He needed cold water to splash on his face… And to fight a powerful urge to taser his colleague.

29

Five minutes of steady breathing and dipping his head in a sink of cold water made a difference. If not exactly calm, Hooley was beginning to regain his humour.

Walking back along the corridor, he became aware that Roper was talking to someone, then he recognised the voice. He was right. As he walked through the door, he found Julie Mayweather making herself comfortable at his desk.

Her face lit up as she spotted him.

"There you are. And I'm glad to see you looking so well. Jonathan was just telling me that this case was putting a strain on you. Something about a speech impediment?" She smiled at him innocently, but her eyes were sparkling, a sure sign she was either angry – or, more likely, suppressing a laugh. If there was anyone else in the Met who knew what working with Jonathan could involve, she was that person.

Dousing the last embers of his rage, the DCI grinned.

"You could certainly say I was lost for words there. Jonathan's unique way of summing things up can certainly have an impact."

Roper seemed oblivious to the exchange, instead focussing intently on his monitor. Suddenly, he clapped his hands. Then, fiddling with his remote control, he made all the screens in the office switch to the same image.

"This is the video feed from Stone and Partners starting a few minutes before the attack this morning."

All that could be seen was the receptionist sitting quietly. She handled one phone call but otherwise all was quiet. Then the attack started. In the frame, the woman was suddenly turning her head and raising her hand to her mouth in shock.

A few seconds later, the lift doors opened, to reveal Gerald Stone standing there. Holding a large manilla envelope, he made straight for the reception desk.

He had clearly failed to spot what was going on, for he took two steps before stopping and turning towards the door, where two men wearing balaclavas had burst into view. Now they were pointing guns at Stone, and it looked as though they were shouting.

Dropping his envelope, he held his hands out in front of him, part warding gesture and part surrender. One of the men ran forwards and grabbed him roughly by the arm, almost dragging him towards the exit.

It was over almost as soon as it started, with Stone and the men running out of camera shot. There was a moment's pause, and the receptionist ran across the floor and into the ladies.

Without asking, Roper rewound the section, and they watched it through again. This time he hit pause at the point where the woman dashed for safety.

Hooley looked at Roper and was surprised to see an unexpected expression. If he didn't know better, he would have said it was puzzlement.

"Something wrong with the brain the size of a small planet?" There was a hint of spite in his voice, which suggested that, although the earlier episode may have been forgiven, it was not forgotten.

"No-one has a brain the size of a small planet," said Roper, his tone dismissive of further conversation. "And there is nothing wrong. Well, not exactly. It's just that... I was expecting to see the brains behind all this."

It was Mayweather who reacted fastest.

"You thought we'd see evidence that Mr Stone is the man the world's intelligence agencies have been looking for?" She paused. "I think that is unlikely."

"Yes. I agree with you now, but that is why I thought it was entirely possible."

Roper slumped back in his chair, a familiar-looking frown appearing, saying nothing until Hooley demanded an explanation.

"Come on. You can't keep us in suspense."

Roper pulled himself upright. "I thought it was strange that they should go back – unless that was always the plan. Grabbing Stone on a second visit would have been a great cover for him. No-one could suspect that he was the brains."

"So why are you now so sure that he isn't responsible?" asked Mayweather.

"It was that envelope."

His two superior officers looked at him inquiringly. "What are you talking about?" said the DCI

Roper answered, "It was an item for posting today, something that seemed important to his business."

"How did you know what was in the envelope?"

"After we spoke to the receptionist, I noticed there was a document sitting in the urgent collection tray. It hadn't been sealed properly, so I looked inside.

"It was a set of cheques that all needed paying into the bank today. Not vital, but important they were dealt with. If you knew you were going to be snatched, you wouldn't risk losing important admin work that needed picking up today. I put it out of my mind because there was nothing of value in it, but it has taken on meaning now he has been taken.

"But the most interesting thing is the way Stone reacts to the men in the balaclavas. He is obviously terrified. He freezes to the spot. His eyes are darting around, but he is unable to move. I think that shows he was genuinely terrified. Not putting it on."

Hooley interrupted. "I seem to recall you telling me that sociopaths are so dangerous because they can lie very convincingly. Maybe he's one of those. It would make sense with this gang and how ruthless they are."

Roper gave him an approving look. "I did say that, and if Stone was that, it would be a vital piece of information. But it doesn't count in this instance."

"It doesn't? Why is that? I thought that Stone behaved pretty badly over the money issue. He seemed to have no empathy at all for the Webb family."

Roper was already shaking his head.

"Being selfish doesn't make you a sociopath. I also assessed Stone, and in my opinion, he is not a sociopath. "More interesting, is going to be finding out the real reason he was so adamant that Webb should not receive any money, only to change his mind when he was under pressure."

30

After Julie Mayweather had gone, Hooley headed off for the main incident room, eager to chase up progress on the CCTV search.

So far, it had been slow. But that was about to change when, out of the corner of his eye, he noticed Roper paying one of his rare visits to the office where teams of detectives and analysts were working around the clock.

Hooley was just wondering what had brought him out into this space when he spotted the reason. A small, blue-haired young woman had just let out a loud yelp after colliding with the corner of a desk.

It was Susan Brooker. She had managed to get to them in superfast time.

Hooley couldn't have been more pleased to see her. Roper said she'd been working on a new algorithm that did something complicated with CCTV… At that point, the details had gone over his head. He did note Roper's assurance that it would make a difference, speeding up the process by which thousands of hours of footage could be checked.

He headed over to where Brooker was rubbing her thigh with one hand and waving off Roper's offer of assistance.

"Susan," he began, "good to see you! And apologies for the close positions of the desks. We've got a lot of people on this, with more arriving. I hope you'll be OK?"

Hooley knew that Brooker had trouble judging spaces. It made her look clumsy, which led people to misjudge just how intelligent she was… Not a mistake made by Hooley and Roper.

Brooker gave him a smile. "The number of times I do this you'd think I'd get used to it. But it comes as a surprise every time. Never mind. I'm here. How are things going?"

He inclined his head at Roper. "I'm not going to sugar coat it… we are up against it. Even our man here is fresh out of theories."

"I was desperate to get here sooner," Susan said, still massaging her thigh, "but I needed to stay while they tweaked the algorithm. It's all ready to roll now – and I hear you've come up with a nice simple task. Find a white van in London."

They exchanged rueful grins.

"At least we have a partial number plate for you," said Hooley. "Where do you want to work? Out here with all the crew, or in with us two?"

Brooker was more social than Roper, but she needed to have space – or else face the prospect of being covered in bruises and the butt of many jokes. It was no contest.

"Definitely with you two. Jonathan can fill me in while I load up the software. If this van is findable, then we're going to find it. This stuff really works. The best mathematician in France has put it together."

They headed back to the office where Hooley, knowing exactly where Brooker would end up, had arranged for a desk with a working terminal to be in place. A few minutes later, she and Roper were deep in conversation – and Hooley, who had found himself drifting upon hearing the word 'software', was left behind. He didn't object; he knew he just had to wait for the result. Besides, coffee was in order, and it was his turn – an easy round since it was three Americanos with cold milk on the side. Since his heart op, Hooley liked to keep track of what went into his body. He wasn't always virtuous, but he tried to be most of the time.

By the time he got back, he was astonished to find Roper and Brooker already studying the first clips of the van they were looking for. By some strange magic – or Brooker's algorithm – they'd found a clear shot of the whole number plate, which was being run-down as fast as the system could operate so that its details could be traced.

"We picked the van up as it approached Kensington High Street," said Roper. "It looks like it was heading East, but it could turn off anywhere."

Hooley felt a shock of anticipation.

"Have you been able to follow their route?"

It was Brooker who answered.

"Your team has been fast in requisitioning the CCTV footage, but there are a lot of gaps at the moment. Those are filling up, but it's nowhere near one hundred per cent."

Their sense of frustration was shared by Hooley.

"For a minute there I thought we might be in touching distance."

He could sense the pair were bristling with tension, they were so close to a breakthrough.

"Be careful you don't take all the responsibility on this; I don't want you to start blaming yourselves if this doesn't come off. You can only work with what you have."

This last was primarily aimed at Roper who could happily heap blame on himself in any situation. All three looked at each other for a moment, before Brooker went back to tapping in some pretty esoteric looking commands.

"Does the software give any estimates about where vehicles will end up?"

"It does – but you have to be careful not to put too much into it."

"OK," said Hooley. "Let's come at this another way. You mentioned it could be heading East. Where would you next expect to pick it up?"

Brooker gave him an approving look.

"That's not a million miles from what the algorithm is doing. Or is about to."

With a flourish, she hit the return key. Her screen went dead, then reappeared showing a map with some blue lines overlaid on it and flashing blue icons at different locations.

"Voila!" she announced with a flourish. "What we have here is a route map of London. The solid blue lines suggest likely routes and the flashing blue icons are where the software is looking for CCTV feeds to establish if the van we are after is heading that way." She tapped her finger gently on a spot in the centre of the screen. "This is where our van could make a series of turns, so if we can find the footage, we should be able to establish which direction it's heading."

Hooley leaned closer, his pulse quickening.

"Is this live? Are we tracking them now?"

She smiled apologetically.

"The program is far faster than we can keep up with. It would just be a blur if we watched it live. Try and understand. If you imagine the software has already checked this area, what we're looking at is a backfilling exercise that shows us what the algorithm is doing." As she spoke, more solid blue lines appeared, together with new flashing icons. She studied the screen. "They headed East along Kensington High Street. That icon shows where they could have made a turn."

They all waited for the next burst of information. Hooley realised he was almost hopping from foot to foot, perhaps he needed to give himself the same lecture he'd just delivered.

The pace was picking up. More solid blue lines appeared with an icon showing a turning for Sloane Square.

"Have we got response teams heading there? I know this was a while ago, but maybe they're around."

Roper said, "I'm passing all the information on. We have four vehicles heading for the area. They just need more instructions from us."

At that moment, Brooker's screen updated with a solid blue line meeting Sloane Square, turning right, and then making another right before stopping.

"They've stopped at Peter Jones, the department store. That's quite clever of them, so long as they keep their faces obscured," said Roper, a look of frustration appearing on his face.

"What's clever about it?"

"When we get the CCTV, we'll see them get out of the van, go into the store, and then just disappear through a different exit. We'll track them eventually. It's a worry to think they may have some idea of how we might be able to track them. Even GCHQ has only been using this stuff for a while, and it's not been reported anywhere."

Roper looked at Brooker, who nodded, and went on, "This particular algorithm was only made available to a few people a short while ago, just days really. So not only are we looking for some seriously clever people – they're getting some seriously major help."

Hooley felt a cold chill run down his body.

"Who else has access to this?"

Brooker took a breath.

"The French, obviously. Ourselves, the US, Germany – and I understand the Israeli security service has its own version."

Hooley whistled through his teeth.

"So, one of our top allies may have some sort of involvement?"

While they had been speaking, Brooker's screen had been cycling through several video feeds. In the final one, a white van had neatly parked up. Hooley watched as the driver and another man got out of the front doors. Both were wearing the infamous clown mask. The pair turned to a CCTV camera and bowed before running into the store.

Hooley swore angrily, but it was Brooker who raised the critical question.

"Where's Stone?"

31

The fast response teams were now just minutes away.

"Anyone else thinks there's the chance we're being played?"

The question came from a grim-faced Hooley, but it could have been any one of them. Even the recently arrived Brooker.

"We certainly need to warn those officers to use extreme caution."

Roper's comments seemed to spark the DCI back to life. Grabbing his office phone, he issued a series of orders.

"I want a cordon set up around that van – and if that means evacuating the store, then so be it. And I want the bomb squad there right away. Until they've inspected the scene, no-one is to approach that vehicle. As soon as the bomb team's there, give them control of the scene until they declare the area is safe."

Hooley glanced over at Roper to see if there was anything else, but he shook his head emphatically. Then he slammed down the phone down and rubbed his face. In a perfect world, he would take a breather right now, go for a stroll and maybe stop off for a pint. He shook his head. Fat chance. This case was on the move. He studied the younger pair. If they felt tired, they weren't showing it. Roper had that look which suggested he was using his Rainbow Spectrum. Brooker was a picture of determination, tapping furiously at her keyboard as she followed the progress of the algorithm.

He said. “It feels like you have worked a minor miracle already. Can it tell us if Gerald Stone is in that van?”

She patted her screen. “This system is good, but not that good. We need someone to go and look.

“In future, who knows? The theory is, it will learn more, the more that we use it. Then it will start to anticipate what we need it to do.” She paused, sensing he wanted to know more. “Take the van. In a few months from now, the algorithm will be pinpointing all the CCTV throughout the area and anything it can’t access it will flash up. Like us needing to get the film from Peter Jones. At the moment, we need to make the request – but soon it won’t have to wait for a human operator to make the call.”

Hooley could see why this might prove controversial. As a police officer, he knew this would be a powerful tool in his armoury – but there was no doubt it was an example of Big Brother.

He gathered himself. Philosophy was for another day.

“My money says Stone is most likely in the back of that van. I’m just hoping he’s not strapped to a bomb.”

Brooker nodded. “That’s as good a guess as we have right now. But in answer to your first question, the algorithm is trying to help in another way.

“It’s currently backtracking over the route to see if the van stopped anywhere and transferred Stone to another vehicle.”

“Now I’m really impressed,” said Hooley, and even Roper was looking thoughtful, as though he was contemplating a mind like his own.

“How long until we get an answer?”

Brooker studied her screen for a moment.

“At the current rate of progress, it will take a little under three minutes. I’ll have a more accurate answer in thirty seconds once the variables have been taken into account."

Hooley decided he just had time to deal with a variable of his own. He needed to respond to an urgent call of nature. Coffee might be great at helping you keep going, but there was always a price to pay. He made a run for it, leaving a bemused Brooker behind.

Moments later, as he walked back, he heard Roper telling Brooker, "A lot of it is down to his age."

The DCI rolled his eyes. Naturally, Roper was right – he simply couldn't hang on the way he used to – but right now was not the time to get into that discussion.

"Was Stone moved at some point of the journey?"

Brooker gave an expressive shrug. "We didn't find anything to say it did stop somewhere, but there is a catch to that – the algorithm can only put an 80 per cent probability on it. It seems there are still gaps in the coverage it can see."

"So, there's a one in five chance we're missing something," Hooley mused. "I've won money on the horses with worse odds than that." He paused. "We're going to have to wait until we check that van – and that reminds me – do we have an estimate on when the bomb squad are arriving?"

"Just a few minutes now, maybe sooner," said Roper.

"What about your algorithm, Susan? How long until it's 100 per cent certain that it's scanned through every bit of footage?"

"That's a bit harder to answer. Some of the footage we need to check is hard to get hold of because it's held in closed systems. Not a lot, but enough to slow things down. If Stone's not in the van, we may have to wait another half an hour or so."

Before the DCI could reply, Roper chipped in, "Bomb squad on site. We're being patched into their communications."

He turned up the sound on his monitor and, moments later, they heard a calm voice.

"Initial scan of the vehicle not proving any data. Blackout glass prevents us from looking inside. Switching to thermal."

Another pause.

"We have a signature that suggests adult human at the rear of the vehicle. Checking doors now."

There was a much longer pause.

"Checking rear doors."

Hooley almost jumped out of his skin at the sudden noise. He'd been holding his breath without realising it and gulped down a lungful of air.

An urgent word from Roper indicated that they had patched into a CCTV feed which allowed them to see what was going on. All the monitors in the room flickered to life, showing two people wearing the distinctive bomb protection gear at the rear of the van.

One of the men moved to touch the door handle...

Hooley felt an icy hand grip his chest as smoke poured from the back of the van. In moments it had totally blocked the view. A man's voice could be heard shouting "Get down. Get down. The view cleared slightly, and for a moment, dim shapes could be seen moving. Then a thunderous roar burst out, and the audio and video feed abruptly shut off, leaving a shocking silence.

32

Things had changed.

For some time now, Edward and Daisy had been allowed to have the light on, and extra food was being provided as well. It was still mostly supermarket sandwiches but, to their joy, they had also been given the means to make tea and coffee.

Edward had just made them both a drink – strong and sweet in Daisy's case – and carried it over to her.

"Like my men," she'd said, trying to cheer them both, but Edward was fifteen and very literal. Despite her attempts to explain, he hadn't really got it.

He'd just handed over her drink when the chief guard came back, this time with another man. The pair brought in a third bed, followed by a fourth. It made for a tight squeeze and, from the expression on the lead man's face, Edward doubted this was going to herald good news.

The man seemed to read his mind.

"I bet you'd love to know what's going on, a nosy little git like you. Well, you'll find out soon enough – but there's no prize for guessing things are going to get a little bit crowded in here. Don't worry, you won't have very long to wait."

Then he sauntered out, leaving the pair looking at each other.

"I wonder who the unlucky people are going to be?"

Daisy had perked up since he'd first arrived. Now, for the first time, she was showing some interest in her environment.

"I was filming when the whole Golden Shot thing started up, but I thought they never had more than two captives at a time." She paused. "What do you think it means that they're bringing in two more people? Are they saying that they've already decided about you and me?"

It was a grim thought and neither wanted to dwell on it, so they sank into a gloomy silence. Edward tried to eat a ham sandwich, but his mouth was dry, and he could barely swallow.

About an hour later, the lead guard was back, looming in the doorway.

"I've got someone here for you."

With that, he made a "come here" gesture with his hand and in walked the handsome figure of Ricky Horton.

Daisy gawped. She'd met him once at an awards ceremony, and the two had not got on. Their relationship had soured even further when Horton told her that, though she wasn't really his cup of tea, he was willing to sleep with her so that she didn't go home disappointed. His resulting black eye was captured by the photographers and, together with the story, had gone viral. Various headline writers had amused themselves with "Daisy the Knockout" and "KO Daffodil."

Daisy gave Ricky a flat stare, then announced, "What the hell are you doing here?"

He shrugged. "I don't suppose you've been getting much internet down here."

Edward's heart sank. He had a feeling that he knew what was coming next. So did Daisy.

"Are we in some sort of competition?"

Ricky looked very glum.

"We are. They want to find out which one of us has the best fans. They reckon that, although we have a lot of followers, we don't have many genuine supporters, people who will try to help us."

"This is worse than I thought," she said. "What happens when they get the answer?"

He shook his head sadly. They both knew what happened to losers on the Golden Shot.

Daisy clenched her fists, unable to take in this bizarre turn of events.

Soon, the door opened again, and a dishevelled middle-aged man was shoved through the door. Edward blinked in astonishment.

"Mr Stone? What are you doing here?"

Stone looked shifty as he recalled the recent row he'd had with the teenager's father, but he quickly recovered. "Edward, I'm so pleased to see you – and, all things considered, in quite a good shape! Your mum and dad are frantic about you. We've all been so worried. We couldn't believe it when you turned up on the Golden Shot."

He stepped closer and winced as he put weight on his wounded leg.

"Are you OK?" asked Edward.

Stone quickly recovered.

"Don't worry, it's nothing. I just bashed my leg when they threw me into the back of a van and drove me here. Wherever here is. Does anyone know?"

It was Ricky Horton who answered.

"I think we're somewhere near the Strand."

The other three turned to him. While it might have been unfair to say Ricky was dim, there was an accepted view that he was somewhat more blessed in the looks department than for his brains.

It was Edward who asked the question that was on all their minds.

"What makes you say that, Ricky?"

33

Hooley jumped to his feet as the explosion ripped out from the back of the van, a dense black smoke cloud enveloping the two men crouching by the rear door.

Even from the sanctuary of their office, the DCI felt the tension like physical pain. He took the welfare of the men and women under his command or acting on his behalf, extremely seriously. And now it looked as though two more people had lost their lives.

The burst of energy that had driven him to his feet faded as fast as it arrived, and he sat back on his chair.

He rubbed his eyes and tried to calm down. There was always a moment when you wished you could just walk away and leave it to someone else to pick up the pieces – but that was not an option. He needed to push the despair away and refocus.

It was Roper who broke the silence.

“The smoke is clearing. I think I can see the bomb disposal team.”

Hope burst inside the DCI. Impossible as it seemed, he too could make out the outlines of the two men. As the smoke cleared some more, one of the men fell backwards, before getting back to his feet.

Contradictory thoughts battled in his head. How could it be that the two men had survived the blast? His eyes told him they were OK, but his heart said otherwise.

One of the men spoke, his voice sounding remarkably calm as if miracles happened every day.

"It was some sort of 'flashbang' device. Powerful enough to stir things up a bit – but not enough to hurt us through these protective suits. We're checking inside now."

The DCI bit down a response to shout out and tell the men to run away. They were safe, and that was all that counted.

On the screen, one of them had pulled the doors open and was looking inside. This time there was no explosion just blissful silence.

One of the operatives came on.

"We have a hostage bound and gagged inside. Checking for booby traps now."

One of the pair disappeared into the back of the van. It was only a short while before he declared the van was safe.

Working together, they carefully lifted the hostage out of the back of the van and laid him down on the tarmac. Two paramedics had been waiting a safe distance away, and – as soon as they were given the go-ahead to enter the zone – they came running up with a trolley. They carefully lifted the hood that was covering his head, cut the ties on his hands and feet and gently lifted him up onto the trolley.

A thick piece of tape had been fixed across the young man's mouth. The moment they removed it, he greedily accepted an oxygen mask, sucking down several deep breaths.

"Who on earth is that?"

Hooley had been expecting to see the corpulent figure of Gerald Stone. But, instead, he could see a far younger man, on whom he had never before clapped eyes.

"They switched him on the way here," realised Roper. "They're playing us for fools again. That's the only possible explanation."

As he spoke, they could see the paramedic team start to wheel the trolley away, heading for their ambulance.

The DCI made an urgent request to talk to the man before he was whisked away to a hospital, but the message came back that he spoke no English.

"Then I want an officer with him every step of the way. I don't want to run the risk of him disappearing before we speak to him." Hooley paused for breath. "As soon as we find out what language he's speaking, I want a translator down at the hospital. Until we establish whether he's a good guy or not, you have my permission to handcuff him to the bed. Just say he's being held for questioning under the Prevention of Terrorism Act. That will do for now. If we need to charge him later, then so be it."

Without waiting for a response, he turned to Roper and Brooker.

"Can someone tell me what just happened?"

"I think the gang were able to monitor what was going on from the moment that van parked up outside Peter Jones," said Roper. "They probably chose that precise spot to give them a CCTV feed. If I'm right, from the moment they left the accountancy office, they have had a plan to throw us off the scent. They made sure that even using the algorithm, we would not have been able to track them fast enough."

Roper took a deep breath because what he had to say next was weighing on him. "I also think this confirms my suspicion that we have a mole – and I now think that mole is based in London. It has to be someone who can access our investigation."

"Do you think it could be someone in this building?" Hooley didn't like the thought, but he needed to ask the question.

"I don't think so," said Roper. "The way we operate probably prevents that. We have a basic grouping, us three, and I'm sure none of us is the mole. Susan is the only person who has just arrived, and I suppose you could make an argument against her."

An indignant-looking Brooker was just about to protest, but Roper rolled on.

"There's no question about her loyalty, and I doubt it is one of the teams working in the main incident room because it is too random. People only get assigned there once we need them. There is no guarantee any police officer would be selected. It depends on who is available at the time."

Hooley could see where this was leading, and sure enough, Roper took the direction he expected.

"If you were going to spy on us, you would want good odds and be able to access our investigation. That means the most likely culprit is with MI5 or MI6. We should check both – but I think it will be someone connected to MI5. Someone who can access the information without drawing attention."

"Why not MI6?" asked Brooker. "And what's making you sure this is the case at all?"

"MI6 operatives move around too much – but, with MI5, there has been a growing movement that sees them looking at organised crime. That increases the likelihood of them making contact with the wrong people. Profits from crime are huge," Roper shrugged, "and there would be plenty to hand around for someone willing to be bought. As to why I am becoming so sure there is a problem… the clue is in their planning. It has been meticulous, and they have anticipated every move we make. That tells me they knew we would bring in Susan for her expertise – and that suggests they have someone aware of what she has been working on. Having someone in MI5 on board would be a big advantage."

Hooley didn't waste time wondering if Roper was right, however unpalatable the theory, he had to take it seriously. He was already trying to work out how to break it to Jenny Roberts. He probably needed to ask for another joint meeting with Mayweather and the spy chief. It would not be enjoyable. Any suggestion of corruption was unwelcome.

"How are we going to identify this mole?"

"I'm not sure," said Roper. "I do have an idea, but it might not work."

34

Ricky shrugged at the question.

"It's that church, innit? The one that plays nursery rhymes."

Edward was struggling to process the celebrity's unusual cognitive approach.

"I'm not sure I'm quite with you. Which church are you talking about?"

Horton shrugged again. "That posh one in the Strand that my nan used to take me to on Sundays. She used to say I needed a few prayers if I was going to have any chance in life."

Edward could see a church in his mind's eye.

"Do you think you can remember what it's called?"

Ricky looked uncertain.

"It was a French-sounding name. Madame Maria, or something."

Inspiration struck.

"Do you mean St Mary le Strand?"

"Yeah. I mean, probably."

"Well, don't worry about that for a minute. You said something about nursery rhymes?"

Ricky looked pleased.

"That's right. Oranges and Lemons."

Edward was about to ask another question when enlightenment struck.

"You mean the bells, don't you?"

As Ricky nodded, the other two looked even more puzzled.

"I read about it last year. St Mary le Strand is one of the churches that play Oranges and Lemons with its bells. Some people think it's the only church which does, so it gets quite a few extra visitors because of it."

Ricky piped up. "That's what me nan used to say. When they brought me here, I heard the bells playing. I've heard them dozens of times over the years, so I knew it was them. We came to a stop not long after, so we must be in the same area. I'm sure of it."

Stone was looking at him in a way which suggested he, for one, would not be trusting anything Ricky had to say. He jerked his thumb at the social media star. "If he told me what day of the week it was, I wouldn't trust him. Anyway, why are you putting so much effort into worrying about where we are? We could be in the basement at Buckingham Palace, and it would make no difference."

Edward had only met Stone a couple of times, so he didn't quite know how to say what he was thinking. He gathered his courage.

"Before you two arrived, one us was going to get out of this – and now we have something to tell the police about where we're being held. Until now, my best guess was that we were still in London – but I had no idea where so that wasn't much help. Now we know it's in the centre..."

Before they could have any further discussion, the chief guard was back, his now-familiar smug expression plastered over his face.

He pointed at the two celebrities. "They want you pair, first. It turns out you'll need to be convincing – because, at the moment, the world seems to think this is a big publicity stunt. Who knows – maybe we'll have to kill one of you to prove this really is life and death, I'd be happy to lend a hand."

He leered at Daisy in a way that made her feel nauseous and made Edward desperate to protect her.

Grabbing her hand, the man pulled her roughly through the door, waving Ricky through behind her.

"You two needn't get cosy either. You're up, after our little TV stars, although I've no idea what they'll make of you. A weedy little kid and some fat, middle-aged bloke. The only way I'd send in money would be to have both of you terminated." He turned to leave, then span back, theatrically smacking his forehead as if to say he'd forgotten something of grave importance. "When your dad tried to borrow the money to free you, Mr Stone here got all difficult about it. He had to be shamed into it basically – but, eventually, he promised to make the money available. The trouble is, Edward, that now he might just need the money for himself..."

35

Hooley was incredulous.

"You want to do what?"

Roper was calmness personified although Brooker was looking extremely doubtful.

"I did tell you that you might not like it."

"Not like it? That doesn't tell the half of it!" Hooley looked down at his coffee-stained shirt. "And you might have waited until I'd swallowed my drink before dropping that into the conversation..."

"I don't think it is that difficult at all. It's the obvious thing to do, in my opinion, so I don't understand why you are making such a fuss about it."

There was a slight edge to his tone, which the DCI couldn't help but pick up on. Roper was moving into what might best be described as his "stubborn as a mule mode." Hooley was going to have to tread carefully to avoid Roper, turning it into an issue from which he refused to back down.

The problem, or maybe 'issue' was a better word, was a matter of interpretation. What Roper regarded as a logical and obvious solution was often beyond the pale as far as other people were concerned.

Roper had announced that, if he was given unfettered access to the MI5 personnel files, he would be able to identify their mole. He was being unequivocal about it, showing no sign of doubt in his own theory.

Hooley had done his best to head it off, arguing that some of the files would be closely guarded, probably defined as important to national security. But it made no difference: Roper was adamant, even after Hooley had appealed to Brooker to intervene.

"You've spent a lot of time working with the spooks recently. What do you think?"

Brooker had sided with the DCI.

"There's no way they'll let you access those files. Even the chiefs have to provide a written explanation before they're allowed to have a look. The French team I've just been working with were a tough lot. They'd probably shoot you for even asking."

Her comments had been ignored, and Hooley knew he was out of options. He either made the request or risked Roper getting bogged down in obsessional behaviour.

He gathered himself. They'd spent enough time discussing it, time they couldn't really afford. Without another word, he picked up his phone and dialled Mayweather's office. Soon he was explaining that he needed an urgent meeting with both women – and only had the briefest of waits before he was told to head over to Scotland Yard immediately.

As he stood up, Roper made to leave with him, but Hooley lifted his hand.

"Sorry, Jonathan, but you're going to have to trust me to do this on your behalf. I'm only going to ask permission for you to see these files, not me and not Susan. While the final decision will be down to Jenny Roberts, I also want Julie there for her advice. They may have questions – questions about you..."

Roper looked as though he had anticipated this response. "You mean, can I be trusted?"

"I do. And have no doubt I will say you are. You can be in no doubt of that."

Roper sat down again. "I'm not worried about that at all. I know I can be trusted and, if there is something secret there, I will never breathe a word of it. Never."

As Hooley sat in the back of the car for the short journey to the Yard, he reflected that he had no problem in believing that Roper could keep a confidence. If the man said something, he meant it. With Roper, no grey areas were allowed.

The two women were waiting for him. They looked calm, but what he had to say would soon impact on that. He glanced out of the window, it was a grey, overcast day, well suited to his current mood.

Mayweather waved him to a seat. "I know you wouldn't have requested this meeting unless it was vital. Why don't you crack on, and we can ask questions after you finish."

As he talked them through Roper's theory, he noted that both stiffened slightly, as though anger was making their muscles clench. He noticed that two spots of colour appeared high on Robert's cheekbones, and his boss's expression changed from stern to angry.

He finished and waited for questions. He was waiting to deliver Roper's request. He wanted them all on the same page before he asked.

The MI5 boss spoke first.

"I can't deny that you have set out a plausible case, but I need your help to take this further. I only really know Mr Roper by reputation. Is it your opinion that we can rely on his intuition since you have no evidence?"

"I do think that. Jonathan has an extraordinary ability to discern events that goes beyond the ability of anyone I have ever worked with. I'm not saying he's infallible, or some sort of mystic. He can, and does, make mistakes – but I think he's onto something here. He's very calm about this, which is always a good sign. The times he's most likely to get things wrong is when he isn't handling pressure well. That has not been an issue in this investigation."

Mayweather spoke next. "As you probably know, Jenny, I also work closely with Jonathan, and I've come to value his insights. He can spot connections that the rest of us miss. What he's saying here may be unpalatable, but you ignore it at your peril."

The spy boss folded her arms. "Thank you for your insights. I assume you have a plan, and I assume I may not like it – but don't let that put you off."

Hooley didn't hesitate. Once he'd decided to make the pitch, he had stopped worrying about her reaction.

"Jonathan, and it would only be Jonathan, would like access to your personnel files. He believes you will have the information he needs to work out who our traitor is."

Roberts' expression didn't alter.

"I cannot possibly allow that."

Hooley was braced for the answer, but it still hit home. Now he was going to have to spend valuable time talking Roper down. He realised that Roberts was looking at him expectantly.

"Sorry, I was lost in the moment. Did you say something else?"

She nodded. "I said I might be able to help. I have had a tight team posted to this case, and I am willing to let him see those files – or, at least, some of them. It's straightforward really – he doesn't have the security access to read everything, so I will have to redact the files he can see. If I get people on the case now, and I will ask them to go gently with what they do redact, it shouldn't take long."

Roberts paused before going on. "There will be some other conditions. He will have to be accompanied while he reads them, and there will be no physical note-taking."

Hooley nodded. This was non-negotiable.

She gave him a conspiratorial grin.

"I may not know him well, but from what I do know, what I am about to say may help you sell him the compromise. Tell him this is my only offer. I will not discuss it further or budge a single inch. I offer no explanation, and my reasons are my own."

Hooley stood up to leave. "I think that might just do it," he said. "I'll let you know what he says."

36

Edward and Stone barely spoke to each other while they waited for the return of the two celebrities. Too separated in age and personality to have anything in common, they sat on their beds, huddling under their thin blankets. The schoolboy managed a couple of sandwiches, his appetite seeming to bear an inverse relationship to the presence of Daisy Daffodil.

Time seemed to drag on and on – even though it was less than twenty minutes before the reality stars were back. Both Stone and Edward were then taken off to a make-shift studio area with a sound mic and powerful lights. This, they were told, was where they were going to shoot their "trailers."

Edward went first and was told to study the autocue to follow his words. It felt like he was cocooned in light with darkness all around. He was scared, it was easy to imagine he was surrounded by unseen enemies waiting to do him harm. His legs were trembling, and he was breathing in short gasps. He hoped he didn't fall over.

Out of the darkness came a loud shout of "action." The words on the autocue were rolling, and he stared stupidly at them, unable to take them in.

The lead guard emerged from the gloom and went to cuff him around the head but was stopped in his tracks as the voice – it was the director – boomed out over hidden speakers.

"No need to rough him up. The way he stood there looking shocked was just perfect. I should have scripted that myself. Let him finish. I'll sort it out in the edit."

This time he was given a countdown so was ready for the autocue. It felt awkward, but he finished, his fear making it hard for him to understand the words he was speaking, despite the director ordering retake after retake. He'd get to the end, and the relentless voice would command: "Again. Do it again." He seemed to make a new mistake on every take. It was exhausting. He was finally allowed to go and was marched back to the cell.

The lead guard shoved him inside and started to close the door when he stopped and turned back.

"Word to the wise," he laughed as he shut them in. "Walls have ears."

"What was that about?" asked Ricky.

Stone, who had returned first, was the quickest on the uptake.

"It means they must have a microphone in here... Or one of us is trying to cut a deal."

Ricky was struggling. "I don't get it."

Stone gave him a contemptuous glance before he went on. "Our guard was obviously implying that they have some sort of surveillance gear in here so they can monitor what we're up to and what we're talking about. But I can't see anything in here." He gestured around the room, and all eyes followed his hands. "Anyone?"

They all shook their heads.

"So, what does that tell us?" asked Stone, not waiting for a response. "It means one of two things. Either there is something in here, but we just don't know what we're looking for – or our guard is trying to disguise the identity of which one of us is happy to sell-out the others."

Stone looked at each of them up and down. "Let's face facts. It's every man for himself in here. We're just a bunch of people thrown together by chance. You can hardly say we're the best of friends, no matter how much bonding we do in this crap hole."

Both Ricky and Daisy started to protest that it wasn't them, but Stone wasn't having it.

"It could be any one of us."

Edward felt compelled to offer an alternative view. "Or maybe they really are listening in," he said, "and they want us to turn on each other."

The conversation died away, and soon they were all left to contemplate their thoughts.

Moments later, the lead guard appeared with a laptop. "Courtesy of the director," he said. "She thought you might like to see how you've scrubbed up, as it were."

Ricky and Daisy grabbed the computer and set it to play. They were first up. They'd been given a script to share, Daisy with the bulk of the lines.

Once again, the camera zoomed in on her red-rimmed eyes. She began talking.

"The Golden Shot is shaking everything up. Ricky and I have exactly 48 hours from now before one of us wins, and the other loses." As she spoke, a digital clock appeared in the top right of the screen and began a countdown. "The winner will be the one who has received the highest amount of donations. It's going to be first past the post. Winner takes all. "If I win, then I have to shoot Ricky to confirm my victory."

The film cut to Ricky.

"If I win, I shoot Daisy," came Ricky's voice.

As the video clip ended, both Ricky and Daisy carefully avoided looking at each other.

Daisy sobbed, "I can't kill someone, not even to save my own life."

No-one went to comfort her; they were all in the same boat, although Edward wondered if he dared wrap an arm around her.

A new clip appeared and went straight to play. Edward came up on the screen.

"Hello, mum, hello, dad. You can forget about raising the money for me." On-screen he came to a stop, choking back a sob. The film carried on. "I'm going to be in a race for votes with Mr Stone. You'll see his picture in a minute, but in 24 hours from now, they count the votes and decide the winner. The result will be announced the day after that."

The screen went blank and then came back to life with a repeat of the murder of William Over.

Edward was just wondering about the clown when he popped up. He bounced around, performing a sickly pastiche of a caper, then leered at the screen.

"To help you make your donations, we have set up our very own website. You could say it's a bit of a riff on those charity sites. Ours is called: 'Just Kidnapping.' And we get to keep all the lovely profits. But a word of warning – even though we've gone to a lot of trouble, you'll need to be quick. The spoilsports hunting us will be desperate to take it down." The clown beamed. "So, there you have it. Full disclosure. It's all change on the Golden Shot. Stay close because we have loads of action for you!"

He wind-milled his arms and the picture cut away to earlier footage of the clown whipping the audience to a frenzy.

"What have we got?"

The answer came back as an ecstatic roar.

"A show to die for!"

37

Hooley had raced back to Victoria, but before he had the chance to appraise Roper of the deal, the alert had gone up as the Golden Shot went live.

The three of them watched in silence as each of the victims was paraded for the viewers. It quickly came to an end, and Brooker was the first to speak.

"I've been looking at social media," she said. "It's amazing how many still think this is some sort of publicity stunt by PR people working for Daisy and Ricky. It doesn't matter how many other people tell them we're watching murder live on air, they just don't seem to get it, or want to get it. I've even seen comments that Mr Over wasn't really killed. The doubters claim the pictures were just faked through digital manipulation."

Susan glared defiantly around the room, looking ready to take on the world. Hooley hid a smile. Not every young person, it seemed, was a paid-up member of the snowflake generation.

Brooker was pulling on her coat. "I need coffee to calm down. Strong and plenty of it. I take it you two will be sticking to your tried and tested choices?"

They both gave her a thumbs up. Hooley said, "While you get the drinks, I'll bring Jonathan up to speed on the deal from MI5. When you get back, let's discuss what we just saw and what we can do about it." He paused. "Oh, and perhaps you could get some of the doughnuts that Jonathan likes so much? We need to keep our spirits up."

The expression on Hooley's face could not have been more angelic. But that was because he knew she liked to subject his eating and drinking choices to intense scrutiny. Occasionally she teamed up with Roper to put the hard word on him.

"Clock is ticking, Susan!" he said as he waved her out. "Grab the brain fuel, and then we can get down to it."

She hurried off, leaving Roper, looking expectant. It didn't take long for Hooley to run through the deal. He wrapped it up by repeating Roberts' concluding comments.

Briefing over, the DCI waited for a reaction. He was anticipating disagreement, but Roper surprised him.

"That all makes sense. Robert's is right to say I don't have the security clearance to read everything. I don't know how far back I need to go. At least a decade for the senior operatives, but I will have some sense of the relevant background material which will allow me to add in details."

Hooley frowned at him. "I'm not quite sure what you mean about background material. I don't think anyone is planning on letting you access anything else."

"Oh, it's elementary, really. Say I'm reading something, and it becomes obvious what date we're looking at."

The DCI was looking more puzzled than ever.

"Think of it this way. Say I am reading a document which gives me enough clues to establish the date. Maybe something that might have happened ten years ago. So, the background material is what I have stored in my memory. All I have to do is pull that out and then I can place the two things together, allowing me to build up the big picture."

Hooley nodded. "I'm impressed. Where do you keep all this information? I sometimes think your brain must be overloaded as it is."

"The brain is a hugely untapped resource. It's not that it is hard to store stuff, it's about how to retrieve it. My

Rainbow Spectrum helps here. I can file lots of historical data and only call it up when I need it."

Hooley was saved from further mind-expanding insights by the return of Brooker who distributed her purchases. Handing over his drink, she offered him a doughnut with a smile on her face.

"Good news. They've started doing a doughnut with fifty per cent less sugar. There you go." If anything, her look was even more angelically innocent than his had been. He accepted it in good grace.

"I'm sure this will be delicious." After taking a bite, he decided it just about passed muster.

After quickly filling her in on the deal, he switched the conversation back to what they had just seen.

"I'll start with the obvious. Our timeline just got a lot shorter. If they stick to it, we now have less than forty-eight hours to stop them."

Roper stood up. "We need to think in a shorter time frame. They're saying they will kill the first victim after forty-eight hours. If we don't free everyone well before that, then they will all be dead. Which brings me to another point." He looked around. "We keep seeing them escalate this. They're moving faster than ever and with more victims. That suggests they are planning something dramatic."

He stopped talking for a minute, looking pensive. Hooley knew that he was running his thoughts through something that was like an internal fact-checker.

"My fear," Roper went on, "is that this all points to them killing everyone. Up until now, some people have been allowed to go free – but that isn't likely to happen this time. I'm wondering if we need to start factoring in what happens to the audience. We've obviously been thinking about the kidnap victims, but ever since this started, I've been trying to factor them in. Who are they? Where do they come from? And how are they being held? I am beginning to fear they will be victims too. They will likely end up being murdered."

Brooker jumped in.

"You're right about the audience. You've just reminded me… While I was in France, I heard a few people speculating that they may have been brainwashed. Maybe even manipulated into behaving like a death cult."

Hooley felt his spine turn to ice. These were thoughts that had been at the back of his mind. Now they had been dragged into the light. Before he had a chance to comment, Roper was talking again.

"I had been thinking about a death cult. It would make sense and make it easy for the people behind this to kill everyone. All the Golden Shot team would have to do is tell them they are heading for a better life and then get them to drink something laced with poison."

Hooley was sweating, despite feeling cold. He wiped the back of his hand against his forehead.

"I think I preferred it when I thought of these people as ghouls. Are you now saying we need to feel sorry for them?"

Brooker was on her feet. "Actually, it may not be a case of feeling sorry for them. Maybe we should be getting anxious. The US intelligence services have been doing a lot of work in this field and new mind control techniques. With the right sort of people, ones who are especially vulnerable, men and women can be persuaded to do anything. They even had an example of a man who set himself on fire with petrol and never said a word as he burned to death.

"I know Homeland is especially worried that terror groups are getting better at spotting people who can be manipulated. It would mean a lot more suicide bombers."

“Are you saying we have a large group of people who’ll be sent out as suicide bombers?” Hooley couldn’t hide his concern.

Some sort of unspoken exchange took place between the younger pair. There were times when they seemed able to read each other’s thoughts.

“We can’t rule it out,” said Brooker. “We don’t think it’s very likely, but it is a possibility.”

The DCI thought furiously, then reached for his phone.

“Julie Mayweather needs to know about this. That’s a significant escalation to the threat level.

“Before I make the call, do you want to say anything else, or change your mind?”

38

Hooley was put through to Mayweather without delay.

"Susan and Jonathan have come up with an alarming scenario. They're both in agreement that the so-called audience in the Golden Shot may be under some form of mind control."

He heard her sharp intake of breath. "What evidence do you have for this?"

He said, "Susan is aware of secret research by top people in the American security services. They believe that new techniques in mind control are proving highly effective when used against the most vulnerable. It raises the possibility that we might find ourselves facing suicide bombers. Obviously, we can't quantify it precisely, but it is something you need to know."

"How many might we be talking about?" The voice was calm, but Hooley knew her well enough to sense the sudden spike in tension.

"We can't be sure. We don't know how many people are in there. Jonathan has a theory that it's about one hundred, but…"

Mayweather needed details.

"I'm going to have to recommend we raise the threat level to 'Critical' and alert everyone from the Mayor to the PM and the security services. I'm going to need everything you've got. I'm going to come to you – I don't want you to waste any time travelling. Expect me in half an hour."

She clicked off, and Hooley stared at his handset. "Well, I think it's fair to say we have her attention. You two have about thirty minutes to decide if there's anything else we need to tell her.

When Julie gets here, I want you," he looked at Roper, "to take the lead. It's your theory that got the ball rolling." Then he looked squarely at Brooker. "But you've got the knowledge which takes this from being a bit of speculation to something we have got to take seriously. Don't hold back with any information you have."

Hooley's phone rang.

"Change of plan," said Mayweather. "Prime Minister's direct instruction, which totally overrules anything I said. The three of you are to address an emergency Cobra meeting at 3.30pm – that gives you ninety minutes. I'm sending a car with outriders as escorts. Get there twenty minutes before. I've arranged access to a small side room where you can give me an outline briefing. It will help me prepare the answers to the questions that are going to be heading my way."

Brooker couldn't hide her excitement at being called into the Cobra meeting. "I've always imagined what it must be like to be at one of those."

Roper was a veteran. "We'll be in a long room with a thin table. The worst thing is how many people can crowd in there. I try really hard to shut everyone out, or I start worrying they are all looking at me."

Brooker smiled at him. "Do those breathing exercises I told you about and remember – our job is to save lives, so it doesn't matter about who is there or looking at you."

The DCI thought he couldn't have put it better himself.

Less than thirty minutes later their car pulled up outside the main Cabinet Office buildings in Whitehall. Little more than a stones' throw from 10 Downing Street.

Cobra meetings are attended by all the key players with a stake in the events under discussion, including senior civil servants and security experts. This meeting was being held in one of the larger briefing rooms since so many people needed to be involved. As Roper had predicted, the room was dominated by a long wooden table and by the time they had briefed Mayweather it was standing room only. There was a babble of noise, but everyone fell silent as the PM walked in. He sat down and called out "Begin".

All eyes fell to Roper who was experiencing a brief coughing fit. Hooley knew it was nerves and hoped he would be OK. He was reassured as the younger man began speaking in a clear voice.

"My colleagues and I believe it is highly likely that the audience for the Golden Shot is being held using some sort of mind control,

"If we are right, they may pose an additional threat. There is research that suggests large numbers of people can be manipulated into becoming suicide bombers.

"We don't have any hard information. This is speculation on our part. But it does help to explain how all those people are willing to sit in the audience. Right from the start, it has been hard to see how ordinary people could be made to behave as these people are."

His words were met with silence before Jenny Roberts said. "If I may, Prime Minister." He nodded, and she went on.

"My team was given a few minutes advance notice of this theory, and we agree. That audience has always been a puzzle, and this does seem to fit the bill. I feel that, unless we prove otherwise, we have to agree."

The mood was already electric, and her words added to the atmosphere. Everyone started talking at once, and the PM intervened. As silence fell, he began taking opinions from around the room. While a few expressed reservations about the lack of facts, no objections were raised to it becoming a working theory.

The meeting broke up, and they walked outside where Mayweather said. "We need to get these people, Brian, and we need to get them before they hurt anyone else."

Hooley nodded. "The way they've been taunting us shows an underlying arrogance. They clearly think they're smarter than us – and that's a big mistake. Up to now, they've been the ones on the front foot, but I get the sense that with Susan here to help Jonathan it will make headway. It may be fanciful thinking on my part, but I fancy we might be about to see how they like it when the boots on the other foot."

39

Roper was about to get in the back of the unmarked police car when his phone rang. The number was withheld, but he answered anyway.

It was the call he'd been expecting. One of the several assistants in Jenny Roberts' office was on the line. The message was clear and straightforward: He should report to MI5 HQ at Thames House, near Albert Bridge, in thirty minutes. "I'll alert security that you will be arriving."

He made his goodbyes and headed off to his meeting. Brooker offered to come with him for moral support. He was tempted; but as Hooley pointed out, she wouldn't have made it inside the building. "There's no plus-one on this ticket. It's strictly invitation only and no-repeat use."

Susan accepted the rejection calmly; she'd had enough experience of the intelligence services to recognise that not obeying the rules always had consequences. It could be irritating – but some secrets needed to remain secret.

Roper set off at his usual rapid pace. With time to play with, he crossed Westminster Bridge to the south side of the Thames, then headed north along the footpath before re-crossing at Lambeth Bridge. As predicted, here, he stopped for five minutes to admire the view from the halfway point.

Even after taking an extended route and making a brief stopover, he arrived ten minutes early. As the official HQ for MI5, Thames House was a hive of activity. As he waited, Roper was able to enjoy the anonymity of the holding area to which he'd been directed.

At precisely the allotted time, a guide appeared. He didn't look old enough to have left school and gleamed as though he had been polished and pressed in some giant machine. Roper didn't notice; he was already thinking ahead to what he would be allowed to read.

Security was slow and thorough, but soon Roper was being led into the depths of the building. As they went, the young man offered no name and made no attempt at conversation. Not that Roper minded. He simply followed, until at last, they arrived at a solid looking wooden doorway with a metal frame. Here a large man was sitting at a small table. He stared intently at Roper, then picked up a photograph, studied it and nodded.

His guide regained his voice.

"You need to hand over any recording services you have. From a pencil to a smartphone. They'll have to be left here."

Roper complied, quickly passing over his phone. He hesitated over his somewhat battered, leather-bound notebook. It was a gift from his parents who had died in a car accident when he was a child, leaving him to be brought up by his maternal grandmother. Roper had clear memories of his mum and dad, but precious little in the way of possessions.

The giant was surprisingly gentle as he extracted the notebook from his fingers, put it on the table and looked up expectantly.

"He needs to search you again, and you'll have to leave your jacket outside."

Second pat-down completed, the guard sat down at his table, and the younger man knocked twice on the door. It opened immediately to reveal a woman in her 40s, black hair pulled back in a pony-tail and oversized black-framed glasses. Her stern appearance was mitigated by a warm smile.

"Thank you for putting up with our security checks. They can be tedious, but they're part of standing orders."

Stepping back, she beckoned him inside. Roper saw it was a small square room, twelve feet by twelve. It had no windows and light came from a large, sealed, ceiling unit. In the centre of the room was a circular table made out of oak, across which two chairs faced each other. On the table were five cardboard files, none of which seemed especially thick.

The woman watched Roper take in the room and the files. The warm smile appeared again.

"I hope you're not too disappointed, but we can only release limited details. Even then, I can assure you that this is a unique event. You must have friends in very high places to be allowed to see anything at all." She paused. "I will be staying in the room while you study what we've provided, and you only have twenty minutes before we must ask you to leave."

Roper needed no further invitation, sitting in the nearest chair and picking up a file. It was the thinnest of the five, and he studied the picture that came with it.

He looked at the woman. "Margaret?"

There was no warm smile in return, just an appraising look.

Twenty-two minutes later, Roper was on the pavement outside Thames House. His escort had waved him outside with a minimum of fanfare. He pulled his phone out of his jacket and called Hooley.

The DCI picked up on the first ring. "That didn't take you very long. I was just talking to a friend, and he told me they weren't thrilled that you'd been given any access at all. There are some seriously miffed people down there."

His comments passed Roper by. He was only interested in what he had seen. “I’m going to walk back; it will give me time to sort through everything I have just read.”

40

The clown was back and at his most unpleasant. The alert about a Golden Shot special announcement had come while Roper was returning to Victoria. He'd just had time to get coffee when it appeared online.

Even though the clown looked no different, he managed to convey an air of gloating triumph.

"I realise that it's been a little while since we bought you an update on the world's worst detectives." He put his hand to his mouth like he was regretting what he said and trying to push the words back in. "So sorry! That's quite unfair of me. After all, we're talking about Scotland Yard's finest. The very best that the Met can dredge up." The white-gloved hand was pressed to the lips once again. "Sorry, so sorry. I get ahead of myself and shouldn't imply that the famous duo Roper and Hooley had to be dragged out to get on the case..."

He looked around.

"Actually, they are no longer a duo. They've had to bring in some outside help in the form of a delightful young lady called Susan Strumpet. No, wait! I have it wrong. Her surname is Brooker. Anyway, the three amigos have been having adventures over the last two days. As well as turning up late for the action, today they got to see the Prime Minister himself. They were with lots of other girls and boys at a Cobra meeting. Poor Jonathan. He was really scared until his girlfriend – Susan – calmed him down." Clown Face paused. "That's it for now – but do stay tuned.

We have another important update coming in an hour from now. So, there you have it. The Golden Shot. A show to…"

"Die for!" screamed the audience.

Hooley turned the volume down.

"That was one big wind-up from the start," he snapped. "I'd like to know how they found out about the Cobra meeting. It wouldn't surprise me if one of those smarmy gits from MI6 was involved."

Hooley had developed quite an antipathy towards the spy agency, which from time to time got the better of him, running the risk that it would affect his judgement. He knew he shouldn't do it, but the antipathy stretched back many years to when a senior MI6 official had been deeply unpleasant to him. The man had sneered when he learned Hooley had not gone to university. "Not bright enough, I suppose." Had been the comment that did the damage.

There was a brief silence until Roper said. "Why are they saying I was scared? I was fine."

"They're pretending that you're stupid," Brooker laughed. "Which is just daft because everyone knows you're not. It's like them saying I'm your girlfriend. I'm not. You know that, and so do I. It just shows that they set a very low standard."

The DCI was feeling lightheaded and realised he hadn't had anything to eat since mid-morning.

"Shall I get some pizza delivered while we talk this through?" Without waiting for an answer, he went ahead and called the restaurant. "Petty insults to one side," he said, after he'd hung up, "they did know about the Cobra meeting and must be feeling very self-confident."

"I've got an idea about them knowing where we were. I just need to run it through my Rainbow Spectrum again and see what other connections there are."

Fifteen minutes later, the front desk called to say that Hooley's food had arrived. Brooker volunteered to fetch it

– she liked running up and down the stairs – and, by the time they had finished eating, the clown was back, flickering on the laptop screen. His opening remarks shook all three.

“Nice pizza chaps. Must admit that I’m partial to a pepperoni myself, especially with the extra chilli.”

Hooley was on his feet. “I don’t know how they’re doing that, but we need answers fast.”

He sat down again; he needed to watch the update, not waste time shouting at someone.

The clown went on, “While you three have been stuffing your faces, things aren’t going so well for Ricky. He’s hardly getting any votes, not compared to Daisy. We’ve decided to keep innovating. If things don’t pick up for Ricky, we’re going to give him to the audience to deal with. That should be fun.”

41

Despite his best attempts, Hooley could feel the pressure being piled on by the gang. Not only were they demonstrating an alarming brutality, but their ability to spy on the DCI and his team was also getting under his skin.

He looked at Roper. "I think this development fits your theory that there may be a leak from MI5, and we'll get back to that in a minute. First up, though, I want to make sure we're covering all the other bases. Susan, you go first. Any thoughts on what we need to be doing? Do you think we might be missing something? Or maybe we could be doing something better? Say whatever you like. The normal rules of the Odd Bods apply. Assume you've got it wrong and maybe you might get it right."

One of the things the DCI liked about her was that she remained rational, even during the most intense pressure. She didn't disappoint now.

"That broadcast is making me think about protection," she began. "You've extended the armed cover to me, as you have for the Webb family and accountancy offices. But what about Ricky, Daisy and Gerald Stone? Are there enough police officers guarding their families? This gang seems determined to keep showing how clever they are and how stupid we are. Well, what about them grabbing Daisy's mum from right under our noses? It doesn't have to be her mum. It could be any family member – or all of them. The same goes for Ricky and Stone."

The DCI went very still. She was right, and he was cross with himself for not having given it any thought.

"Well done, Susan. I've taken my eye off the ball. There are officers attached to the family, but none of them is armed. I can't cover every single family member, but I can look after the immediate family."

She took his thanks in her stride. One of the things she loved about working with Hooley and Roper was being allowed to ask questions and make observations.

Hooley made some notes and then nodded at Roper. "Your chance to show us what's going through that galactic sized brain of yours."

Roper pursed his lips. "I do not understand why you persist in saying I have a brain the size of the galaxy – that is ridiculous. I simply use parts of my brain more efficiently than other people do." He gathered his dignity. "I suppose you are going to tell me that it was all a joke."

He ignored Brooker, who seemed to be having a sudden coughing fit. "Well, I suppose a little levity never hurts – but I think we need to remember why we are here. So, with that in mind, I have several concerns. I remain convinced that there may be an attempt to poison the Golden Shot audience.

"I know that sounds a jump but look at the way the gang is operating. They're taking more people, challenging us at every turn… It feels like we are in some sort of end game. If I'm right, then it makes sense that the audience is in danger. These are not the type of people who are going to leave loose ends.

"It's a bit of a long shot, but we ought to put a team on checking if any poison has been stolen. I think that the simplest way to kill a large group would be poison. We know that in the past, indoctrinated people have been persuaded to imbibe drinks laced with something lethal."

He paused, looking worried. "What if they have something like that Russian nerve agent that was used in Salisbury, novichok? Do we also need to alert the National Health Service or the Ministry of Defence? I'm not sure what they can do if we don't know what the poison is, but maybe a warning will help. We need to make checks throughout the country, particularly factories that might need to keep large stockpiles and may not have realised some has gone missing."

Hooley found the suggestions alarming, but it was Brooker who first spoke.

"I think issuing an alert is a good idea, and it may have already been done. It would need to be done quietly; otherwise, you would terrify the country. I do agree about poisoning, and everyone needs to know you think that, but let's get a perspective.

"Novichok is very dangerous and complicated to make. As bad as this gang is, I don't think it is possible they have the expertise or access to a specialised lab."

Roper didn't argue the point, clearly accepting Brooker was right but Hooley could tell he wasn't finished. The DCI was prepared to bet that the younger man was about to run through every aspect of his current thinking about the case. Sometimes that meant he went over old ground, but this was a key part of the way he processed lots of details.

"Thank you, Susan," he said, by way of acknowledging her point. Then he was back on the charge.

"I have suggested this before, but I am convinced that they are somewhere in the central part of London… most likely underground. By that, I am thinking about large basement areas, perhaps more than one floor deep."

Hooley said. "Just to be sure… This is what you believe to be the case based on what little we have been able to observe. By that I mean, you haven't spotted some detail the rest of us have missed?"

"Yes, of course. And drawing on my own reading about London's forgotten spaces. Quite a few of them are to do with ancient rivers. It's not just the River Thames."

Hooley said. "When you talk about the centre can you be more specific?"

"Not exactly – but I do have some thoughts, which I am basing around the kidnapping of Edward Webb. We know he was inside a van which had been parked outside his home. While we don't know which way they went, I have been going through all the witness information, and there is a report from a driver who rang in yesterday. She says she saw a pair of white vans make a right turn against the traffic flowing out of Kensington Gardens. She says they stood out because there were two of them. At that stage, they were heading towards central London."

Sensing objections Roper held his hand up. "I know that it's not much, but I have a tiny bit more. About ten minutes later a pair of white vans were picked up by traffic cameras near Green Park tube. They were briefly on the wrong side of the road, heading towards Piccadilly. After that, they cross into the area around the Strand, and we lose them. It could be, they just separate, or they go underground.

"If it was me looking for a good place to hide I would choose the area bounded in the east by the Inns of Court and Fleet Street, to the north by Tottenham Court Road, the west by the Piccadilly – and the south by Waterloo Station."

Hooley wasn't totally convinced but could see how Roper had arrived at his view. He said. "That's a big area, but it's somewhere to focus on. Let's see where we get to. Julie will be more than happy to supply the manpower."

Roper said, "It would help if we got some people looking specifically at underground spaces, and similar."

"Good idea. Anything else before I go and rustle up a small army?"

"There is. We're going to need Tom Phillips and his team."

Hooley was in instant agreement. The SAS Major had worked with them many times and was a huge asset. Despite their different backgrounds, he shared a powerful bond with Roper.

Hooley put a call in and asked for the Major to call him back, urgently. Then, he stood up and headed for the main incident room, stopping in the entranceway.

"What are you two going to do?

Roper replied, "I need Susan's help going through the MI5 details."

42

Brooker waited for Hooley to leave before speaking.

"I was amazed when I heard that you'd been given access to MI5 staff files. I think, if I'd asked for that in France, they'd have fired me on the spot – with a spell in prison for good measure."

"I was surprised as well," said Roper. "I calculated there was a one per cent chance of them agreeing to my request. I just thought I had to ask."

Brooker had been pacing around the office, but now she perched on the edge of her desk, looking thoughtful. "That's interesting. Do you think there might be some sort of message there?"

"I do. I suspect that Jenny Roberts shares my concern. She couldn't say anything openly, but I think letting me read the files was intended to send out a message. I have been careful not to read too much into it. It could be that she can't rule it out, rather than actively ruling it in."

"I agree," said Brooker. "You have to be very careful about making assumptions when it involves spies. But you were back from your briefing quite quickly – I take it most of the files were redacted?"

Roper snorted with laughter. "You might say that. There was barely a whole page of exact details, and the rest was padding about MI5 itself. It didn't even include real names. I was given the first names of Peter and Paul for the two men and Mary, Melanie and Margaret for the three women."

It was Brooker's turn to laugh. "I doubt if even those are real. Peter, Paul and Mary… That was the name of one of my grandparent's favourite bands." She snorted with laughter. "But enough of that. We both know that dealing with the intelligence services is never easy. Brian's always teasing me about checking if I still have all my fingers after I shake hands with what he calls one of the 'spooks.' How do you want to play it?"

"I've memorised everything that matters, so I will just tap it out. But there is something you can be doing in the meantime... I was thinking about it on the way back here, and it is a bit odd. The file on 'Margaret' – well, she was actually there. She was the woman assigned to watch over me while I read the files. There was a picture of her as a teenager, and there was no question it was her. She just ignored me when I asked, but she was too unresponsive, not moving a muscle. It's a mistake that a lot of people make when they are determined to give nothing away."

"That's very interesting. Do you think that Jenny Roberts has her doubts about this woman?"

"It did cross my mind. Look, if I give you a few details, can you start digging for information? She was born on June 12, 1980, with the family home in Kennington. She went to the City of London School for Girls, won a scholarship to Baliol, Oxford where she studied Classics, graduating a year early, in 2000. After that, she was picked up by MI5 and allowed to delay starting for twelve months so that she could take up a short-term scholarship with the Cairo Museum."

"A lot of spies in Cairo," said Brooker.

"I wondered about that. But then I thought about London. There's a lot of spies here too, and criminals, and terrorists… You name it, they are all here."

"Good point. I'll get digging on her background and see what comes up. Perhaps we'd better do some basic work on all five, then decide if anyone looks more likely than the others?"

"Agreed," said Roper. "We must not allow ourselves to be influenced by the way Jenny Roberts has presented the information. Clearly, she can't be that sure herself. Maybe it's to do with her being unable to rule her out, rather than rule her in. And, if that is the case, she has to be very careful about how she presents her thoughts. She can't say anything directly because, without clear evidence, that would be seen as her being willing to throw her under the bus at the first sign of trouble. At the same time, if she has doubts, then she has to find some way of expressing them."

Brooker looked at him admiringly. "You know, I'd forgotten how much I enjoy working with you. Life is never boring when you're around."

The pair spent the next hour silently working, with Roper filing his reports from memory. At the same time, Brooker plugged in a search algorithm that she had "borrowed" while on secondment at the Washington base Homeland Security. At the time, she couldn't quite believe what she'd done. Only after six months, when no-one had arrived to arrest her, did she relax enough to think about how she could use it. With the help of a friend, she'd been able to make subtle changes that limited some aspects of its searchability. Making it harder, she hoped, for anyone to spot what she was using.

What she was doing was risky, very risky. It wouldn't be good if anyone in authority found out she had the software. But then security services all over the world would probably go into cardiac arrest if they knew just how many of the "geeks" they employed had a habit of sharing technical information.

As they worked, Brooker couldn't stop herself glancing at Roper. Did he know what she was doing? He was usually quite rigid about right and wrong but could be very adaptable when it came to catching the criminals. Then he seemed to take the attitude that, sometimes, the end can justify the means.

A thought occurred to her. Roper had never asked her for details about how she got her hands on super-secret software packages. This was a surprise, given how much he loved detail in every aspect of the rest of his life. Maybe he was being practical. Roper had contacts everywhere and knew all sorts of secrets. Perhaps he was taking the view that, by not asking, he was making sure he was never able to give away her secrets.

Talking of which, she checked another programme she had running. It was a clever piece of work that could spot if anyone was tracking what she was doing. Brooker could feel her back starting to ache so rolled her neck to ease the pressure. At that moment a warning symbol popped up on her screen, almost making her fall off her chair.

"Jonathan… Someone's tracking us."

43

Hooley's requests for extra officers were met with instant approval. It was going to take time to get everyone in place. So, he and the Incident Room Inspector had worked out a rough guide to who received protection first, which was immediate family, then moving outwards.

In a perfect world, he would have found protectors for everyone at the same time, but that was never going to happen. In the end, however, he was content that the plan they had come up with, making the best use of resources, would eventually ensure everyone would be contacted.

That was more than could be said for the attempt to find out if any poison had gone missing. It turned out there were a great many industries that used deadly poisons in small quantities – and many ways of stealing it. What he'd initially thought of as a potential lead was going to be time-consuming. In the end, he left it up to the discretion of the Inspector.

Frustrated at the mixed results, Hooley was walking back to catch up with Roper and Brooker when his mobile rang. It was Tom Phillips.

"I'll be with you in five minutes. Maybe less, given the speed, my driver's doing – maybe more if we have an accident..." Hooley heard the SAS Major shout loudly; then he was back on the line. "That was close, a sliver of paint job! Anyway, we're still moving... Now, I don't know what it is you and Jonathan are onto, but it trumps a top-secret,

'I'd have to kill you if I told you' mission for the Foreign Office. They've had me shut away for days, so I have no idea what's going on in the real world.

"Anyway, I showed them your text message and, the next minute, the top man himself is ordering me out of the building and to take his car. So here I am – whoa, another close one! Those double-decker buses are big beasts when you get right up alongside them!"

Hooley couldn't help laughing. "I'll tell security to let you in, the moment you arrive. You know where we are," he said. "See you soon."

With a renewed spring in his step, Hooley headed back to his office. Roper was thrilled that the Major was on the way. He and Roper had forged a powerful bond and worked well together, each one an expert in their own fields and each having total trust in the other.

Hooley's mobile rang. It was Phillips. "I'm outside and, after that ride, coffee is in order. I take it that you two are still on Americano's with cold milk?"

"You need to make that three drinks. Susan's here as well."

Fifteen minutes later, the Major let out a low whistle. "I was aware of this Golden Shot but thought this was all happening on mainland Europe. The media coverage barely touches the edges of what is going on. I hadn't realised that the focus had switched to central London. No wonder they have you guys on it. From what you're saying, we're dealing with the worst sort of people.

"What might be helpful is that other job you rescued me from… I had two teams lined up. I can put in a call to switch them to this."

"I think we can all guess you're going to get a positive response to that," said Hooley. "Jonathan. What do you want to do?"

"Keep on doing this. It might be a good time for you and Tom to sort out some details while Susan and I keep our database searches rolling along." Roper frowned. "We have another problem which you haven't heard about yet. There's a mole, and there is a good chance they are with MI5. That means they might be accessing all the available information. We've got some possible candidates – so Susan and I are trying to narrow things down as much as we can.

"To make it even worse, Susan just found someone trying to access our network. They were clever and managed to escape before she could backtrack, but it shows what we are up against."

The Major looked grim. "If it is someone at MI5, there'll be hell to pay. What can I be getting on with, in the meantime?"

Hooley replied, "I have an idea, but it depends on how long these two are going to be. A couple of hours?"

"Sounds about right," said Roper.

"In that case, why not come with me while I speak to the Webb family, the ones whose son was snatched outside their home? I want to see if they can remember anything else that might be linked to their son being taken. You can make your calls, and I will have a chance to brief you in more detail."

Roper was nodding enthusiastically. "I had talking to the couple again on my list of things we need to do. If I didn't have this to go through, I'd come with you."

"I'll do my best to be a good stand-in for you," said the Major, and followed the DCI out of the door.

As they walked down the stairs, the Major was smiling. "I love it when I hear from you guys. If nothing else I know things are going to be interesting."

44

The visit to the Webb family drew a blank, the couple seemingly becoming confused amid the intense pressure.

At one point, Mrs Webb appeared to be under the impression that her son, Edward, was merely late home from school. Continually checking the clock and telling anyone who would listen that he "should have been home by now." Meanwhile, her husband was also showing signs of losing his self-awareness.

Hooley quickly called it a day, not wanting to add to their misery.

"If they do know anymore, they're not in a fit state to pass it on."

"I agree," said the Major. "I don't think you had any real choice. I'm no expert, but they were acting like some soldiers do when they've been in one firefight too many… Post-Traumatic Stress Disorder seems to be the most common description. These things are hard enough for the military to cope with, and at least we have some training. It just isn't meant to happen to civilians."

On the journey back to Victoria, they talked in more detail about Roper's theory that the show was being beamed out from somewhere in central London, possibly underground.

"He's managed to put together a good case. There's a lot of underground spaces in that area."

The Major nodded. "Aren't there some old tube stations that have been abandoned, and Churchill had a huge bunker during World War Two, big enough to allow him to run the country from."

Hooley waved this away. "No-one can spend their entire time on a state of full alert. Not even you boys. You make a very good point, though. We've massively stepped up the number of beat officers operating in the area Jonathan has roughed out."

"Glad to be of service. And I have another thought for you. If I get the OK to transfer my two teams to this operation, I could even make my men available to go and look. I don't think we have much choice but to get out there."

The Major clicked his fingers. "Actually, I have another idea. At this moment, we have no idea who this mole might be. Until you come up with some leads, why not get my team to check out places like the abandoned tube network? If we keep that information strictly between ourselves, we will avoid details leaking out. The last thing we want is to give these people any warning that we're about to turn up. Brian, my boys are pretty good at hunting through hidden spaces. We learned a lot of lessons chasing the Taliban through the cave system in Afghanistan. And don't get me started about looking for Isis leaders! They're very keen to hide out in cities, using civilians as human shields."

Hooley could feel the familiar sense of excitement that preceded action.

"Well done Tom, I think that's an excellent plan."

The Major didn't need any prompting, grabbing his phone and punching in a short number. It was answered almost immediately.

"Meet me outside Temple Station. We'll be in civvies but bring firearms." That done, he ended the call and waved his phone. "You should be able to get me on this, even if we're underground. But I will make sure to keep checking. I'll call you when we've been through Temple station. I was in there a few years ago. There were worries about a rogue bomber which turned out to be a near thing. There's a surprising amount of space down there. We'll need to cover it all."

He gave Hooley a mock salute and made his way to meet his men.

45

Brooker stared at her screen and saw that the algorithm was starting to throw up some useful data. At first, it pulled together every item it could find. But the smart part was the way it could break that down again by changing the search terms itself; without waiting for operator intervention.

The trick was not to allow it to do all the work once the heavy lifting was done. There was still a need for the human touch, although Brooker often wondered how much longer that state of affairs would carry on.

A few minutes later, all her thoughts of AI taking over the world were overtaken by a nagging worry. She checked again and then braced herself. She and Roper had made a mistake.

"We should have been focusing on Margaret right from the start," she breathed. "Your new friend, Jenny Roberts, was right to put her under the spotlight."

Roper had gone very still.

"Have you discovered who she is?"

She nodded. "I have – and there are three different names for her."

That grabbed his attention, as she knew it would.

"How certain are you?"

"I'm going to be totally sure in about ninety seconds."

Roper understood. "You're waiting for the passport photos, I take it. I have some excellent photo recognition software if that helps?"

She smiled. "What you've got is based on something I've got. There's no practical difference between the two."

Roper looked like he might be about to make something of this when she held up her hand.

"The pictures are here. Do you want to come over and take a look?"

Roper hurried over to her desk. The printer was already gently humming as it came to life. It would be producing three headshots imminently, but Roper preferred to view images on a screen – finding them sharper with better detail.

Brooker leaned slightly to the right as Roper leaned in, being as careful as usual to reduce physical contact to a minimum.

She had arranged the three pictures, in a row, across the centre of the screen.

"Meet Debbie Fairchild," she said, with a sweeping gesture. "All three of her."

Roper pointed straight at the one in the middle. "That's the one dubbed Margaret. She was the one who watched me go through the documentation while I was at MI5."

At that moment, a message scrolled across the top of the screen. It read:

ALL THREE ARE A 98% MATCH

Roper stared intently at the pictures – as if, Brooker thought, he was trying to find the truth behind the images.

All three were of the type used for passports and driving licenses. The picture that Roper had identified from the MI5 office showed an unremarkable-looking woman with her dark hair tied up in a bun, held in place with chopsticks.

The second showed the same woman with a prominent white streak in the centre of her free-flowing hair. Brooker thought it made her look like Cruella De Vil, the streak having the effect of dragging the eye away from her features. An expert wouldn't be deceived for a moment, she thought. Still, it would do a reasonably competent job, especially at busy passport checks.

In the third photo, she was wearing blue framed glasses and big, dangly earrings, beads in her long blonde hair.

Brooker broke the silence.

"It's amazing what a difference a few changes can make. When I was in the USA, I was invited along to a presentation by one of the CIA counter surveillance teams. They said the key to effective change was to keep things simple."

Roper came out of the trance he'd dropped into.

"What do you think this is telling us?"

Brooker didn't hesitate. "There are only two possible options: Either those are MI5 approved, or she's got a couple of spare passports that no-one knows about."

"My money's on the latter," said Roper. "Why would someone working in the main office need secret IDs?"

"Just playing Devil's advocate, but maybe she used to work in that area and has now moved on to a management role."

He shook his head. "I don't think so. Those pictures are up to date, within the last three years. And, even if it was the case that she used to work in that area, her bosses would have shredded any dodgy documents straight away. The view is why place temptation in front of anyone?"

"I'm convinced. What do you want to do now?"

"I'll call Brian and get him to talk to Julie and Jenny Roberts, she'll have the answer, but if we're right, she is not going to be happy about this."

"Well, while you're getting the ball rolling, I shall get the coffee and doughnuts going. See you in a minute."

As she arrived back with the drinks and food, Roper told her that Brian Hooley and Jenny Roberts were on their way.

"Jenny has insisted that everything we have remains here. She's bringing a team with her."

A few minutes later, the MI5 boss marched in, accompanied by two unsmiling women who did not make eye contact. Brooker had just taken an oversized bite of her doughnut and nearly choked as she tried to swallow it.

"Show me." Roberts wasn't standing on ceremony, even matching Roper for abruptness.

The man himself didn't bat an eyelid, simply gesturing that she should look at Brooker's screen.

There was no disguising the look of fury on the spy chief's face as she studied the three images. She beckoned over one of her assistants who produced a memory stick, onto which Brooker quickly copied the images she'd unearthed.

It only took moments, but that was enough time for Roberts to regain control of her emotions. Roper did, however, notice that a small, raised, vein had appeared on the right side of her forehead.

Taking a deep breath, she thanked both Roper and Brooker, then said, "I take it you picked up on my somewhat cryptic suggestion that this was a woman to focus on?"

"I did, although I must admit that we lost a bit of time because, I insisted, we keep an open mind about the mole."

She waved this away. “Have you unearthed any connection to the Golden Shot gang? Maybe they found some leverage to blackmail her?”

She stopped and took another breath. “I’m wasting time. Reasons can come another day.”

She turned to her two assistants. “By the time she walks out of that building tonight, I want the best team, you can assemble waiting for her outside. I want her mobile bugged, I want her flat searched immediately and surveillance installed. I want another team digging for data and you can…”

She trailed off. “I don’t know why I’m telling you how to do your jobs. Go!” Then she waved them out. “I hate traitors,” she seethed. We’ve got enough problems as it is without creating more.”

46

The chief guard was back, accompanied by a couple of equally leery looking men. Standing in the doorway, he shouted at Daisy and Ricky.

"Get a move on the pair of you! The boss wants you, so hurry up."

They were quickly marched away, Edward staring after Daisy long after she had disappeared from view.

"Where do you think they're taking her?"

Stone rolled his eyes but felt some sympathy for the teenager.

"You'll just have to wait for her to come back. In the meantime, be grateful they're leaving us alone. I really don't want to play with that lot."

Edward was still managing to keep track of time and, when Daisy came back, he calculated she had been gone for half an hour.

"What happened? Are you OK?"

Daisy said, "I'm totally fine. I don't know why they wanted me at all. I was taken off to another room just like this and Ricky went somewhere else. I thought he'd be back with you guys."

An hour went by, according to Edward, and there was still no sign of Ricky. The mood among the captives turned even darker. Conversation ground to a halt, with no-one wanting to speculate about Ricky – although their imaginations were doing an excellent job for them.

The heavy silence was broken as the guard came back.

"You're wanted again, Miss Daffodil."

"Where's Ricky? What have you done with him?"

This prompted the unpleasant laugh. "You'll find out in a moment." He looked at Stone and Edward. "You two next. So, don't go wandering off anywhere. I'd hate to have to come looking for you..."

At the same moment, Daisy was walking out, an email was sent from the hidden server on the Dark Web.

By now, millions of people had signed up worldwide and checked their devices as the message popped into view.

"Update from the Golden Shot in five minutes."

Hooley swore under his breath as he read it. Jonathan called up the website, and there was a tense wait before the cacophony blared out. Moments later, there was the sinister clown. He danced around, clearly revelling in the limelight.

"Time is running out here on the Golden Shot – and it seems to be running out very fast for Ricky Horton. It seems as though only his mummy and daddy cares about him – because just £20,000 has been pledged to save him. The fund for Daisy, meanwhile, has topped a million – and the cash keeps pouring in! There doesn't seem the slightest hope for Ricky – so join me in making sure he gets the send-off he deserves."

The clown bounded around as the audience bellowed and jeered.

The shot changed to show a terrified looking Ricky securely tied to the post. He looked bewildered, and the watching Hooley hoped the TV star was oblivious to what was likely to happen next.

Sure enough, the clown was back.

"As you all know, we like to make it interesting here on the Golden Shot – so, like we promised, here's Daisy Daffodil. The big question is – is she going to be able to take the shot that confirms her victory? We'll be back soon with the answer. Oh, and don't forget, we still need to find out what happens between Gerald Stone and Edward Webb! The Golden Shot, a show to die for!"

As the clown went off air, Daisy was marched into the arena.

"Let me be the first to congratulate you on having such loyal fans," the chief guard told her. "They've really turned out for you and voted with their wallets. All you have to do now is kill Ricky, and you're home free."

Daisy felt her knees buckle as the words sank in.

"You must be joking? I can't do that to him. He's just like me. Not important, just someone who got lucky because the camera likes them..."

He shook his head.

"I hope you don't think you have many options here. You either do this, or you die. You won't be saving him. He is definitely going to die… Whatever you do. The only person you can make a difference to is yourself. Do this properly, and maybe you get to live. Or maybe you don't. But at least you get a chance, which is a lot more than most people."

Daisy felt her blood turn to ice. She knew she had been backed into a corner and wasn't sure what she was going to do. She hoped she had the courage to refuse to pull the trigger, but she was badly frightened. It kept crossing her mind that she would be sacrificing herself for someone who was pretty much a stranger.

While she was thinking, the guard received a telephone call. He stepped away into the darkness to take it, careful to ensure she didn't hear any part of the conversation.

When he returned, he had a grim expression on his face.

"Right you are, Princess. Things to do and people to see. There's a bit of a change in the running order – so back you go. But don't worry, you'll be up soon enough."

47

The latest update from the Golden Shot had briefly cast a cloud over the investigating team. Even Roper had lost a bit of his bounce and Brooker was bashing at her keyboard.

Roper looked up and noticed Hooley's raised eyebrow.

"I'm missing something important," he offered by way of explanation. "It feels like I am very close. If I could just reach out, I would be able to take it. Maybe eating something different will let me see what I'm missing."

If anyone else had said that, the DCI would have had trouble not laughing. But he felt himself brighten at these words. When Roper said he was close to some new insight, he genuinely was.

He glanced at the clock. They had less than sixteen hours left of the Golden Shot imposed deadline. He crossed his fingers. He was at the point where anything that might help would be considered.

Roper suddenly stood up. "I've been an idiot. I can't believe I missed something so obvious."

Brooker and Hooley looked at him expectantly.

"I've just realised what's been bothering me. The acoustics. All those short videos that have been put out, if you listen you can hear they're slightly muffled like they're underground."

"Hooley felt a rush of excitement, now they were starting to move.

"I'm calling Tom Phillips. He's due to go into the War Rooms any minute… he needs to know this."

His call was answered on the first ring.

"Jonathan says he is 100 per cent sure they are underground. He can tell by the acoustics."

The Major gave a tight laugh. "Anyone else and I would wonder. But tell him well done. The good news is that I have both my squads, and we all have our weapons. If there's anyone who feels like a fight, I think we can help them out on that front.

"We might be a while. I was talking to the engineer here who reckons the whole complex is much bigger than anyone realised. With all the wartime secrecy, no-one ever had a full set of plans. The point is – it might be the ideal place for these people to be holed up in. From what we've seen so far, they're well-resourced and connected. So, it's not impossible; they found some information hidden away somewhere."

Hooley shook his head. "I couldn't agree more with you checking this out. Not trying to tell you how to do your job – but do you need any back-up?"

The Major laughed. "No worries on that front, Brian. Just about everyone who's had the training has turned up. Including some of your boys and girls. I've trained a few myself. We're moving in a few minutes. With so many people here, we've set up a mobile communication unit so you can be updated on progress. Still, I'll try and call you myself."

The DCI ended the call, feeling some optimism return. A detective appeared in the doorway.

He jerked his thumb over his right shoulder. "Working with the team next door, Sir. We think we might have something on that request you put out for reports of poison being stolen."

The DCI was suddenly alert. "Go on."

"A little over six months ago, a report was filed by Lincolnshire police that 500 grams of Arsenic had been taken from a company that makes homeopathic medicine."

Hooley was astonished. "They use poison in making that stuff? Isn't Prince Charles a fan of that?"

Roper had been listening in. "He values it as part of an alternative approach to staying healthy. Not just homeopathy, other strategies as well."

Hooley filed away the thought that Roper might move in more exalted circles than he imagined. "But why would they need poison?"

"That's simple," said Roper. "It's used in minute quantities, ones that have been extremely diluted, to make a range of remedies for things like digestion or sleep disorder."

The detective sergeant was nodding along in agreement.

"That's right, sir. This production facility is tucked away in the middle of the countryside. They ordered a new supply of arsenic because they were nearly out of the stuff. It arrived and, within forty-eight hours, it had been taken. It was reported straight away but never got any real attention – until now. I spoke to the manufacturer, and they are mystified. They keep arsenic under very tight security in a special safe which the thieves opened with no trouble. In the fifty years, they've had the facility, no-one has even attempted to break in, let alone take something."

With his update made, the man departed. Hooley turned to Roper and said, "I cannot imagine any circumstance in which I would willingly ingest arsenic."

Roper actually laughed, which was a most unusual event. "When I said the arsenic was very diluted, I meant to the point that it barely amounts to a trace. It would be pretty much undetectable and certainly wouldn't do you any harm. So long as you got it from a reputable supplier."

Hooley still looked doubtful but decided to put his thoughts about alternative remedies to one side. "Do you think this supports your theory that the audience is facing being poisoned?"

"I do. It's the only report we've had, and as you heard that detective say, that was the first theft in fifty years. We know this Golden Shot move has been planned for some time. I bet they'd had their eyes on the facility for quite a while."

A brief sense that they might be finally getting somewhere was dashed by Brooker.

"The Golden Shot is doing an update in five minutes."

Hooley shivered as he looked again at the clock. There were just fourteen hours and fifty-three minutes left.

Time was slipping away.

48

Back in the cell, Daisy and Edward watched Gerald Stone being taken away. The reality TV star slumped on her bed.

"What happened?" asked Edward. "I thought they might have made you shoot poor Ricky, or at least try and make you..."

She looked miserable. "I'm sure that was the plan, but for some reason, there was a change."

"Change? What change?"

"I don't know. I'd have said if I'd known!" Fear made her almost hiss with impatience, and the teenager recoiled in shock.

"I'm sorry. I didn't mean anything by it."

He looked so crestfallen she managed a weak smile.

"Look, Edward, this is a bad situation. I really appreciate you asking after me, I really do – but, as that horrible man Stone says, we all need to look out for ourselves.

Her words helped him a little. "You're right," he said, "and I've been thinking about that. I just don't know what to do, apart from hoping that my dad comes through for me. He always likes to say… 'There may not be many of us, but the Webb men get the job done'."

She gave him another weak smile. "That's a nice thought, Edward. Hold on to that. My mum always says that the men in our family are bloody useless."

They both lapsed into silence, each unable to lift themselves out of the fog of depression thickening around them. Neither would say it, but both felt that the end was near.

Almost ten minutes passed, with no sign of Stone or Ricky returning, when Edward was hauled away again. This time, a different guard dragged him to a small room with harsh electric light and a grubby wooden chair. The whitewashed walls were patchy and yellowing with age.

Grunting something about the chair, the guard soon left him behind, and Edward decided that he might as well sit down. Counting in his head, he'd reached eight minutes when the clown walked in.

Edward rocked back in fear, almost toppling to the floor as the front legs of the chair came off the ground. The clown studied him for a while, adopting a so-called "thinker's" pose, holding his chin with his right hand.

Eventually, he spoke. "It seems we have a bit of problem with you – or rather our viewers do. People are complaining that you're too young." The clown paused. "Actually, how old are you? Fourteen, I'd guess?"

Edward managed a brief show of defiance. "I'm fifteen, actually."

"Fourteen, fifteen, even sixteen. It's all the same. You see, the point is, the people watching think you're too young to be killing people – and too young to be killed." He put his hand on his chin again. "For the life of me, I can't think why anyone squeamish would want to watch our show." He flickered his white-gloved fingers like he was catching dust particles. "So, what's the answer? How do we play this? We do like to give customer satisfaction on the Golden Shot. What do you think, Edward? What do you think is for the best?"

For a moment, Edward forgot where he was. "You should let me go. You should let all of us go."

The clown responded with a slow shake of his painted face.

"Dear Edward. There you go again, saying the first thing that comes to mind without thinking it through. We can't possibly let everyone go. Otherwise, what would be the point of the game? You must never take the mystery out of your story. That would never do." The clown shook his head. "But I do have an idea. Let us put it to the vote. Our watchers can decide. That's the democratic way to go about it."

He walked behind the chair and placed his hands on the teenager's shoulders, saying, "up… up" to indicate he wanted Edward on his feet.

"Time's a-flyin', as they say. Let's go. You need to meet your adoring public. I do hope it goes well for you, Edward. I really do."

*

Back at Victoria, Roper had the images from the Dark Web running on the wall-mounted monitor. The awful music announced the Golden Shot was back – and then the camera zoomed in on a frightened-looking Edward Webb. The shot held for a moment before the clown bounced into view.

"Have we got something extra for you! In a moment, I'm going to give you four options for young Edward. Option one – he doesn't have to kill Gerald Stone if he wins the cash battle. Option two – he doesn't get killed if he loses the cash battle. Option three – he does have to kill if that's the result. And option four – we release him back to mummy and daddy!"

The clown paused, seemingly for dramatic effect, then leered at the camera. "Now, I do need to tell you that each text will cost £1, and I keep all the money. Ain't life grand when you get to call the shots?"

As he was speaking, four options rolled across the screen. The screen split to show a slumped Edward on the left and the numbers on the right.

Then, just as suddenly, the clown was back. "Would you believe it? We have our first response – and it's good news for Eddie boy. Our first watcher wants him released."

He pressed his hand to his ear as if listening.

"Well, this is interesting. People are voting – and we have another ten results to tell you about. Bad news for Eddie this time – all ten wants you dead."

49

Hooley couldn't believe what he was watching, anger making him clench his fists so hard that only the fact that his fingernails were so short stopped him drawing blood.

"What must his parents be thinking if they're watching this? It's monstrous… He's just a child."

An equally shaken Brooker was staring aghast at the screen.

"Look at the numbers of people voting. They're showing the running total, shooting up. People seem to think this is some sort of game. Do they imagine that, at the end of it all, the victims get up and announce they were only play-acting?"

Roper seemed to have withdrawn into himself, and Hooley realised he was going to have to calm down for two reasons. The first, he wasn't doing himself any favours. And, secondly, because he knew from experience how hard Roper found it to process emotions. He'd be doing them both a favour if he calmed down and focussed on the job.

But his patience was about to be tested to the limit, for in that same moment both he and Roper received an email.

It was Roper who opened it first. To begin with, Hooley was relieved to see the younger man actively engaged – but that evaporated when he spoke.

"It's a message from the Golden Shot people. They've attached a video."

Brooker, who had been listening in, looked alarmed.

"Don't open it on your server," she said. "Send it to my personal account. I've got the latest GCHQ approved anti-virus on board. The enemy might be good - but they're not good enough to defeat that."

Moments later, they were looking at the clown.

"Hello, you two. You've been assembling your little alliance I hear. First Susan Brooker and now your very own SAS pal, Major Tom Phillips, is on board as well. Good luck with that – you're going to need it. Don't forget, time is running out."

The picture faded.

"I'd really like to slap that clown!" exclaimed Brooker.

"Me too," said Roper.

Their comments brought a tight smile from Hooley.

"If it was down to me, I'd shoot him. He's just winding us up, making it seem like he's all-knowing when anyone could have worked out that Susan and Tom are with us. I also need to find out how the Webbs are. I want them to know we haven't given up on their son, and we are doing everything in our power to try and get him home. I'm going to speak to the liaison officer and then we need an urgent recap, see what else we need to be doing." He paused. "Jonathan, I hate loading you down, but we need your brilliance if we're going to get through this. We've only got until almost midnight before we hit their deadline. It's not impossible that we may have less than that. They keep changing the rules to keep us off balance. We need to do our best to cut out the off-stage noise and keep doing our job. Yes, time is tight, but we can still do this."

It was a rousing speech, especially for Hooley, who wasn't sure where it had come from. He decided he liked the sentiment – if nothing else.

While he was waiting to be patched through to Edward's parents, he noticed Roper was on the phone. As his call connected, he heard Roper saying, "Hello there. Could you put me through to Maria Morton in Peter Webb's office, please?"

Before he could hear more, he was through on his own call as the liaison officer described the reaction of the parents after the segment about their son. Mrs Webb had reacted as if she'd been shot, falling straight to the floor, and Mr Webb had broken into sobs.

"As luck would have it," the liaison officer explained, "the doctor was there and had brought some tranquilisers with him – something like Valium only better, apparently." The man hesitated. "Sorry, sir. The point is they're both knocked out, but not for long. It will start to wear off in a couple of hours."

Hooley thanked the officer and broke the connection, becoming aware that Roper was giving him an expectant look from the other side of the office. He spread his hands in a "tell me" gesture.

Roper leaned back in his chair. "What's that expression that you are always coming out with?"

Hooley hissed in exasperation. "Come on, Jonathan! We don't need to play games right now. Tell me what's on your mind."

Unabashed, Roper announced, "Follow the money. One of the first things you said to me was, 'never forget to find out who's getting their hands on the money."

Roper had his attention now, and Brooker's for good measure.

"Go on," they said simultaneously.

"I've been a bit slow on this. But there has to be a firm that's handling the money that the Golden Shot is making – how to look after it, protect it, keep it hidden. It takes a special accountant to do all of this without making a fuss and attracting attention. And, meanwhile, we also have an accountancy firm in West London where two people have been directly linked to the Golden Shot…"

Hooley interjected, "Are you suggesting that Webb's involved? They've got his son and are threatening to kill him!"

Roper shrugged. "Another thing you told me – never assume anyone is innocent… But no," he said. "I didn't think that at all. In fact, I was wondering about Gerald Stone."

This time it was Brooker's turn to interject.

"He's also facing the prospect of being killed."

"Are you sure?" said Roper. "I just checked, and that counter they have running shows a huge majority of texters are voting for Edward to be killed. It's running about five to one in Stone's favour."

Brooker's eyes widened. "You think they might be rigging it? That Stone is all part of this?"

The DCI was briefly lost for words. He could see a horrible logic at play.

"Anything else?" He finally managed.

"Yes. Peter Webb's assistant, Maria Morton. I just spoke to her."

Now it was Hooley's turn. "Correct me if I'm wrong, but a DI interviewed her, and she said she was going to stay with her mum until this sorted itself out. She said something about not being able to stand being there on her own."

"Exactly," said Roper. "When I called, I didn't say who I was, but Maria was still there – and she sounded very efficient."

Hooley rubbed his hands together. "I suppose she might have missed being at work. But let's get down there. I think I have a few questions for her. Who's coming with me?"

“I think Susan should go. I think Stone may have been moving money around and Susan is one of the best around at tracing any money laundering activity.”

“You’re clearly thinking Stone is working with the Golden Shot people to hide money,” said the DCI.

“I think that maybe the case. There are millions of pounds at stake so they would need expert help with that.”

Brooker chipped in. “They’ll have shipped the money offshore, then moved it all over the place so that it is hard to find – except by me.”

Hooley was on his feet. “Are you coming, Jonathan?”

“No. I’m going to get in touch with Tom. I don’t think he’s looking in the right place. I have an idea, though. I just need to do a bit of work here to narrow it down.”

Hooley thought of objecting to the idea of Jonathan Roper joining the hunt for a dangerous gang but stopped himself just in time. With the SAS team, he reasoned, Jonathan would be as safe as possible – and the time for prevarication was long in the past.

50

Sitting in the back of the unmarked car racing towards Shepherds Bush, Hooley thought about the Webb family but dismissed any thought of stopping off at their home. Time was far too precious to use up on anything less than essential.

He turned to Brooker who was staring intently ahead, clearly deep in thought.

"What do you want to do when we get there?"

"I was just thinking about that. In a perfect world, we'd do one of those FBI style operations where we hit everything at the same time. But we don't have enough expertise for that, this time."

Hooley had rounded up more than a dozen detectives, and they would each have a role to play in making sure everyone stayed away from their computers. Still, financial investigators were rather thin on the ground, especially at such short notice.

Brooker went on. "Given we have to choose Stone's office as an obvious target, we don't want to miss Webb's office and his PA. I think the best bet might be if I focus quickly on Stone's office and you go and keep an eye on Maria Morton. If Jonathan's suspicions are right, she may well hold the key to this."

"Anything you want me to look out for?"

"If she shows any signs of trying to use her keyboard, you need to stop her immediately. When I've done these raids with the FBI, we have a warrant that allows us to arrest anyone who tries to interfere with our investigation."

"I can make that work," said Hooley. "I can arrest her on suspicion of conspiracy and then argue about it later. In the meantime, she'll be in handcuffs and going nowhere."

"I like your thinking, boss."

"How long will it take to find anything, or is that one of those 'how long is a piece of string' questions?"

She shrugged. "The honest answer is I don't know. These things used to take days and days."

"Which we don't have," said the DCI.

Brooker's phone pinged with an incoming message. As she read it, she grinned. "We may not have time, but we do have friends with some rather nifty software. It's been designed to catch drug dealers, people smugglers and the like. It's brilliant at sniffing out money that has been moved around. Some say it can even penetrate the most secure bank systems… But I wouldn't know anything about that."

"I bet you don't," said Hooley with a grin.

She grinned back. "I'm like an open book. The point is, if someone has taken their time and really done this properly, it will take a lot longer. If we're lucky, they'll have followed the usual routes, and we'll be on them in no time. Say an hour."

Hooley nodded and noted they were nearly there. The plan was to hit the building fast and secure the offices. The DCI and Brooker would separate and then re-join.

Minutes later, Hooley marched through the door of Peter Webb's office and shouted at Maria Morton.

"Stand up and keep your hands away from the keyboard!"

She ignored him and went to make some keystrokes – but, instantaneously, Hooley reached across and grabbed her wrist, ignoring her protests.

"Maria Morton, I'm arresting you in connection with a conspiracy to pervert the course of justice."

She stared at him dumbfounded as he slapped on a pair of handcuffs but quickly regained her composure.

"What's this all about? You can't arrest me for doing my job!"

Hooley wondered how many people he'd seen declaring their innocence down the years. He was always surprised at how innocent even the guiltiest could look.

"If you really want to help yourself, then cooperate," he barked. "There are lives at risk here – so you might end up with blood on your hands."

Watching her closely. Hooley was gratified to see, that alongside a mixture of defiance and fear, was the calculating look that came over people who are trying to work out how valuable their information is. His heart lifted. It looked like Jonathan was right. He told her to sit down and wait.

Ten minutes later, a bright-eyed Brooker ran in, nodding approvingly when she saw the handcuffed PA.

"I take it she tried to do a bit of tidying up? The search is on. They've got surprisingly good internet security here. Rather more sophisticated than you might find at most small accountancy firms. Makes me wonder why." As she spoke, she indicated Morton with a nod of her head. "Did you tell her that I spent 18 months with the FBI's money laundering section?"

A quick shake of the head.

"Did you tell her that I'm considered quite an expert?"

"Not yet. Although I'm thinking of mentioning it."

"What about my success rate of tracing laundered money?"

"No, I didn't."

"OK. Well, it's ninety-nine percent."

"That's good. I'll bet she's dead impressed about that." Hooley looked thoughtful. "I suppose I ought to mention that, if she doesn't give us something before you find something, then she's in even more trouble?"

"You probably should mention it," mused Susan, "because I don't think we have long to wait."

A sheen of sweat had broken out on Morton's forehead. Hooley didn't think it would be any time at all before she started talking.

51

At MI5 headquarters, surveillance target Isabella Hardy turned down the opportunity to take a lunch break, saying she was feeling nauseous and would be better off skipping a meal.

Just before 2pm, she complained that she was feeling worse before she started visibly sweating. Minutes later, she only just made it to the ladies where she was violently sick. She stayed in there long enough for concerned colleagues to phone the medical team, where the duty nurse sighed, grabbed her supplies and came into the toilet to find Hardy looking dishevelled and grimly refusing to leave the cubicle.

After thirty minutes, she'd managed not to be sick again, and a little colour had come back to her face. The nurse reported that she had stopped looking feverish.

After another fifteen minutes, she was recovered enough to clean-up, have her blood pressure and temperature taken – both normal – and agree with the nurse that it would be best to go home. "Drink plenty of fluids and, if you feel hungry, stick to plain food," was the advice.

The nurse walked with her to the exit, at which point Hardy declared, "I only live at Kennington so I might walk home. I don't want to get caught on public transport. Thank you for your help, nurse. That can't have been pleasant for you."

The nurse waved her away. "Don't worry about it in the slightest. It's all part of the job, and I've seen far worse – trust me."

Standing on the pavement, she watched Hardy walk south over Lambeth Bridge until she was out of sight, then returned to the building.

Had she seen the spring in the step that appeared once Hardy reached the opposite bank, she might have been impressed at her speedy recovery. London's air wasn't famed for its recuperative qualities.

While the nurse could no longer see her, plenty of MI5 employees could. The moment she had stepped outside, she had been picked up by a significant security detail that ordinarily guarded the Prime Minister. Three teams of six people had her under close supervision, each one rotating with another so that she never became familiar with the faces of individual watchers.

Some hundred metres further back, another operative was checking the incoming reports against the readings of a low-level transmitter that the nurse had slipped into her handbag. The size of a fingernail, it had enough power to last for twenty-four hours.

Back at MI5, Jenny Roberts was in a secure room where the information was being updated continuously through multiple feeds, including video and audio channels.

A watcher reported, "Target is approaching Waterloo Bridge."

A moment later, the same voice reported, "Target has stopped and is trying to look around in a casual manner. Clearly trying to spot a tail. Team B walking on, team C to pick up. Tracker team moving up."

"She's on the move again. She's heading north on Waterloo Bridge."

The comms went quiet for several long minutes; then, a new voice came on.

"Target has descended to Victoria Embankment and has stopped to sit down on empty bench seat. She's checking her phone."

At MI5, Roberts was just thinking she might be waiting for a contact when a voice came on to assure her the observations teams were on the case.

"Microphone planted on the bench seat. If she is meeting someone, we'll pick up any conversation."

Five minutes later, it was clear that Hardy was staying put – and hopes mounted that she was indeed meeting a contact.

The news was relayed to Brian Hooley, who stepped out of the office where an anxious Maria Morton was sitting.

Beckoning Brooker to step outside, he told her the news. She nodded. "Maybe things are heading our way at last. We just need our Maria in there to realise she's out of options and start talking… Then, maybe, we're in with a chance."

Hooley glanced over at the office where they were holding Morton. He had a total of twenty officers, uniformed and plainclothes in the building, all going through files or keeping an eye on staff movements.

"Penny for your thoughts, boss," she asked him, noticing the direction of his gaze.

"I was thinking that it's just as well that hitting suspects is frowned upon nowadays."

On the Victoria Embankment, the surveillance teams had set up a video feed, and Roberts was able to see the situation via a high-resolution colour feed.

As she was admiring the quality of the feed, one of the watchers came on.

"Female pedestrian has just completed what looks like a walk by. She's turned and is walking directly towards Hardy. Stand by."

As the new entrant got closer, the camera picked her up and zoomed in. Roberts felt her heart starting to pump as she studied her closely. She was dressed entirely in black.

“Who are you?” thought Roberts, even as her people took the image and began searching every available database.

52

Roper had been working at a stupendous rate as he checked and double-checked databases against each other. He was especially interested in traffic and security cameras, plus any privately operated CCTV to which he could gain access.

He was so absorbed in his work that he ignored people walking into the office and talking to him. This was going to be one of those days when he added to an already formidable reputation for being the most aloof man in Scotland Yard. Not that he cared. Especially when he was getting close to his target.

Muttering something inaudible, he looked up and was momentarily nonplussed when he couldn't see Hooley. Then he blinked, as he dropped back into real-time. He left a series of messages for Major Phillips, who was still checking out the Churchill War Rooms, then rang the DCI.

Hooley listened carefully and decided that good news did indeed come in threes. It sounded as though the younger man had worked out where the Golden Shot was being transmitted from. They might yet be in time.

Then his natural caution kicked in as he reminded himself that Roper could easily get carried away.

"Under no circumstances do you go in there without Tom," he said. "Wait somewhere close-by but out of sight." Then, sensing that Roper's enthusiasm could get the better of him, he added. "Keep reminding yourself that we're dealing with some very dangerous people who won't hesitate to kill anyone who gets in their way. I wish I was with you, Jonathan, but your suspicion about Maria Morton has proven correct. If she doesn't start talking soon, then I'll be amazed. Now be safe, and brilliant work in finding them, just wait for Tom and his men."

Roper had a car waiting outside and flew down the stairs in his haste to get going. Jumping into the back of the dark blue Jaguar, he told the driver to head for the High Courts in the Strand.

"It's close to where we need to end up, but not so close we'll attract attention."

As the car raced off, he tried Tom Phillips again – but still had no luck. He stabbed the off button in frustration.

They'd just raced past Trafalgar Square when his phone buzzed. He was relieved to see it was the special forces soldier.

"Hi, Tom. I've got good news."

"I gathered you needed to talk to me. I didn't realise it was possible to be on the end of so many missed calls in such a short period of time."

Roper ignored him. "I know where they are. They're underneath the old Aldwych station."

"Are you sure? I never doubt you, Jonathan, but I just wasted time searching the old War Rooms in what I thought was a sure-fire bet."

"I can see why you thought that. I looked at quite a few places before picking Aldwych. I even thought about the tunnels underneath the Old Vic."

"So, what made you focus on Aldwych?"

"I knew it needed to be very central, but the big thing was access. They would need to be able to get in and out without anyone noticing. That was the thing that clinched it."

"Hang about," said the Major. "Aldwych is right out there in the open. There's no way you're getting there without attracting attention."

Roper was in his element. "You're right. That's what made me realise it is perfect. I checked street camera images and the buildings nearby are going through a massive redevelopment."

"Sorry, I'm not with you..."

"Over the years, there have been all sorts of attempts to develop Aldwych – it used to be called the Strand, by the way. Lots of digging has been started and then stopped. Some of the buildings nearby have access to the partially built areas underground. It makes a great place to hide because it's totally in plain sight. No-one would believe the Golden Shot was down there."

"No-one except you," Phillips laughed. "Right, let's get down to business. My boys and I are in our wagons and heading your way. See you in a moment..."

When Phillips pulled up, Roper leapt out of the car, clearly ready for action. The Major held up a hand in warning.

"I know you want to go in with us, and I will allow it – but only once we've checked the area. This is not up for debate, Jonathan. It's going to be dangerous and, if I manage to damage the brightest mind in Scotland Yard, I'll be done for. I'll spend the rest of my career guarding the North Pole."

To his surprise, there was no protest.

"I've realised I don't like guns, so I'm happy to leave all that to you."

They spent the next couple of minutes going through what Roper had discovered.

Photographs showed that right next to the now-closed station was a large Victorian property. Which had been totally gutted so that only the exterior walls had been left behind. Even the floors had been removed, and it was supported by scaffolding.

Next to it was another, similar building, but this one had lost its front-facing wall.

"This is where they've been gaining access," said Jonathan. "Driving inside, then making their way into the basement area and, from that, I think they are accessing the abandoned parts of the station."

"That all makes sense," said the Major. "I'd been wondering how they got into where they were operating from, and also where they were keeping that audience."

"I may have some good news about the audience," Roper answered. "I've been looking at that, and I think there are fewer people than we imagined. Probably around twenty. They've been using all sorts of audio tricks, mixing in another audience to make it seem more."

"That's good to know. A lot easier to deal with twenty people rather than two hundred. "Any more thoughts on who they are?"

"I'm not sure – but I think we are looking at the type of people who don't have anyone looking out for them. That area attracts a lot of homeless people who would fit that bill. Vulnerable and won't be missed. It's a shifting population with people coming and going all the time."

The Major was itching to go.

"Let me brief the troops, but it won't take long. The plan is: Get in and rescue everyone… shoot anyone who gets in the way."

Roper admired the plan's simplicity.

53

The woman in black sat on the end of the bench and pulled out her phone, pointedly ignoring the rogue MI5 agent.

The spy chief spoke to the team leader.

"It looks like they've had enough training to make an effort at counter-surveillance. Just hang on for a while. I'm hearing that facial recognition is closing in on a result."

It took nearly ten minutes – and all the while, the two women looked at their phones – but, finally, a relieved Roberts was back on the line.

"Pick them up. The new arrival is a Verity Wade. She studied film directing at the Royal College of Art. Was considered to have a great career ahead of her but just dropped from sight. I guess she went down a different career path."

The teams moved in, and the two women were grabbed with a minimum of fuss. In under sixty seconds, they were on their way to MI5 HQ, where Jenny Roberts was waiting.

She was going to do the interrogation herself, but first, she phoned Hooley to update him. He'd just heard from Tom Phillips that they were going into the abandoned tube station.

Ending the call, he told Brooker. "The good news keeps coming."

"I wonder if Miss Morton realises that the time to strike a deal has nearly run out. In truth, I'm wondering what she can possibly add that we won't get from someone else."

Morton had clearly reached a decision.

"I can show you the money trail and tell you who came up with the plan."

Both investigators stared at her.

"We're all ears," said Hooley.

"You need to pick my daughter up. She's only two, but they threatened to kill her if I didn't do what they said."

Brooker was frowning. "I don't recall anything about a baby daughter."

"It's complicated. Her dad is married, and if his wife found out I was pregnant, she'd know it was him. Don't ask how – she just would. I promised to keep it secret and to be honest, I was never attached to the baby. Not at first. So... my lover found a family who wanted a baby and made all the arrangements. I was happy enough at first – it was only later I realised what I'd done. I thought there was nothing I could do, but then I got a visit from this man. He had some pictures of my daughter. I was terrified, even before he made the threats against her..."

She sat up straighter. "If you want my help, you need to go and get my daughter – and the people looking after her. He threatened them too!"

Hooley didn't hesitate. "Give me the address. I'll have officers on the way immediately."

She gave them a location in south London, not far from Crystal Palace.

"It's going to take half an hour, give or take. If I take your cuffs off, can I trust you?"

"Don't worry, Detective Chief Inspector. I just want this over. Do you think I could use the loo?"

Hooley looked around. "I don't have any female officers available." Then he looked to Brooker herself.

"Would you mind going in with her? I'll be right outside. I know we're all now friends, but let's not get carried away."

The trio made the trip to the bathroom, and Brooker went inside with Morton, who disappeared into a cubicle. It seemed like she had barely locked the door when Brooker was alerted to her screaming "help me".

Hooley reacted fast, running in and smashing the door aside. He was in time to see Morton hanging by her fingertips from the window, out of which she'd climbed. With a scream, she vanished from view. Looking out of the window, he could see her unmoving on the ground. It was only the third floor, but it was high enough to break your neck in a fall.

"Why did she do it? She was going to make a deal, there was no need."

The DCI was infuriated and saddened in equal measure.

"I don't think we're going to find a baby at that address. At least, not hers."

"But I still don't understand why..."

"My guess is that she was more frightened of someone else than she was of us. That's what made her desperate."

Looking out of the window again, he saw one of his men supervising the body. An ambulance was already on the way.

"What a mess," he sighed. "But you and I need to keep going. Are you OK to carry on?"

Brooker waved him away with a weak smile.

"Don't worry about me, plenty of time to worry later. I need to see what the algorithm has thrown up."

She went off to make her checks, leaving the DCI to curse himself for falling for Maria Morton's little trick. He should never have let her out of the handcuffs. Even if they proved she was in it up to her neck, there would still be trouble.

He sighed. The one advantage of getting older was that you learned to accept that crap happened. He would park that one for now. There were bigger fish to fry.

At that moment, a wild-eyed looking Brooker handed him a piece of paper.

"You're not going to believe the name written on there."

Reading it, Hooley gave her an incredulous look. "You're joking… I hope."

She shook her head. "I wish I was."

"Bloody hell. This case is going to be the death of me." He looked at her suspiciously. "Any more surprises for me?"

"Nope."

"In that case, we need to talk to Roper. In fact, we need to talk to everyone – and fast!"

54

Tom Phillips had two teams of SAS troopers and a full team of armed police officers under his control.

Phillips himself would be leading his men into the underground areas. Meanwhile, the police would be in charge of securing the perimeter areas, in anticipation of the fact that gang members might pop up unexpectedly. They would also be responsible for minding Roper until it was safe to bring him deeper down. The SAS major understood how important it was for Roper to be involved at the end. And he deserved it; without his input and insights, it was unlikely any of them would be here. But, even so, he was determined to keep him out of harm's way.

There was no time to track down any maps of the area into which they were going. He and his men would have to trust their instincts. Phillips was relaxed about this particular aspect of the situation. Detailed plans were all well and good, but any soldier could tell you that battle plans lasted only as long as it took to engage the enemy.

He regarded his men for a final time. They looked impressively fearsome with their black combat armour, masks and variety of weapons. Many had opted for variants of the Heckler and Koch machine gun. SAS troopers chose their own weapons, and the H&K was also favoured by the police. It was a tried and trusted weapon – no-one wanted to go into a fight with an experimental firearm – but Phillips himself preferred a lightweight version of the M4. It wasn't that it was demonstrably superior to other weapons; it just felt right in his hands.

Roper had the protective kit but no weapons. He had been offered training but had turned it down because he found guns frightening.

The Major checked his watch and was again surprised at how fast time seemed to run through your fingers when you were under pressure.

It was 7pm – just five hours before the Golden Shot deadline expired.

"I don't think we have five hours left," said Roper, who had watched the Major checking his watch. "I am sure they want us to believe that, but they are probably getting ready to kill the hostages – and the audience – now."

The Major took a deep breath.

"Then it's business as usual. Shoot to kill."

"There is no choice. Everything these people have done proves beyond doubt that they will kill. I've run the options through my Rainbow Spectrum – and that still confirms how dangerous they are. Even if killing serves no option, there's a danger they will do it."

Roper was far from your typical "gung-ho" cop looking to make a name for himself as a tough guy. Whenever these issues come up, his words were supported by cold, unforgiving logic. The Major had worked with him enough to know that every word had been weighed and considered before he spoke.

He turned to the assembled men.

"You heard the man. The people we're going after are as dangerous as they come. If we can take them alive, then that's all good, but if you have any concerns, then we need to take them down."

As they headed underground, the Major thought it wasn't the most conventional talk about the rules of engagement, but at least it was the most honest.

They were soon in total darkness. Thankful they were wearing the latest generation of image intensifiers, a set of goggles that replaced the pitch black with a bright green light. No one enjoyed using them, but it was like you could suddenly see in the dark.

It didn't take long for them to arrive under the building next to Aldwych station. They'd gone down two flight of stairs so far, and now they followed a route that had been cleared of rubbish and approached a substantial breach in a wall, easily big enough for them to walk through.

On the other side was another set of steep stairs heading down into darkness.

The Major used his radio to talk to the police sergeant in charge of the surface operation.

"I believe we're about to step into the footprint of the station. This area needs to be secured after we move through. I'm leaving two men here. Can you send a team here to take over? I imagine Mr Roper is chomping at the bit. He can come down this far – but no further than the wall breach until I say so."

The officer acknowledged his instructions and added, "I wouldn't like to say Mr Roper is driving me mad – but he certainly is keen to get in on the act."

55

Hooley quickly prioritised his calls. While it was essential to let Jonathan know what Brooker had just shown him, he had to do something first.

Contacting the Duty Inspector at Victoria, he issued a stream of instructions and updates. His first order concerned the Webb family.

"Don't let that man leave. As soon as we finish this conversation, I'm heading to Kensington. I want to make the arrest myself, but if he causes any problems, slap the cuffs on and tell him he's being detained on conspiracy to murder."

"As soon as we finish this call, I'm on my way. Can you get Jonathan Roper and patch him through to me? Your final call needs to be through to Julie Mayweather on the special direct number. Tell her what's going on and say I'll be in touch as soon as possible."

The Inspector, Peter Cuthbert, interrupted. "If you don't mind me saying Sir, this is an astonishing turn. I've worked with you and Jonathan Roper on many occasions on really major cases. Still, I can't recall a development like this."

The DCI could hear the unspoken question… "Can you be totally certain that you have the right man?"

He thought for a moment before answering. "I hear you, Pete. And it is incredible. But the evidence seems clear. Edward's father is directly involved in this. I was shocked myself, but the evidence is clear. Susan Brooker has found financial documents that establish a link between Webb and this Golden Shot operation. It looks like he was helping them launder money through offshore accounts. All the evidence was well hidden, If it hadn't been for Brooker's algorithm, we might never have found it."

Inspector Cuthbert greeted this news with a low whistle.

"I know old hands like myself like to say you see it all in this job,,, but I think that caps the lot. The way he's used his son's predicament is just appalling. I look forward to seeing him in handcuffs."

At the other end of the line, the DCI grinned fiercely before replying. "Well said. I intend to bring Webb into Victoria, so I'll be able to grant your wish in the next half-an-hour." He paused. "Before I go, any news from MI5?"

"I was just about to call you. Isabella Hardy has asked for an immunity deal. They're deciding what she can be offered."

Hooley scowled at his phone. "I'd lock her up and throw away the key."

"I rather think I agree, sir. But, as usual, we may have to hold our noses. Strictly between ourselves, the film director they've picked up is a tough operator. She hasn't said a word, won't accept a drink and even spat at Jenny Roberts. A real charmer by all accounts."

Before dashing off, the DCI went to doublecheck with Brooker. He found her looking pleased with herself.

"Good news?" he asked.

"You could say that. I got through their security like it wasn't even there."

"That is good. Are you still happy for me to leave you here?"

"No problem at all. Someone's got to follow the money, and I would be no use to you when it comes to arresting people."

“That’s fine. I just wanted to make sure you’re OK. There are plenty of police officers here. I’ve told them that they’re to treat you as their commanding officer.”

Susan laughed out loud. “There’s an irony in there, somewhere. I’ll try not to let it go to my head!”

With that, she immediately went back to studying the financial documents she had uncovered.

*

Hooley was so angry that he took the steps at Launceston Place two at a time. The PC on duty held the door open and, marching inside, he went straight into the sitting room. He found both Webbs seated. They looked groggy, presumably from the sedative, but not so bad that he couldn’t talk to them. The wife looked totally lost, but he thought Peter Webb had an expectant air, as though he realised the game was up. Something about the atmosphere must have alerted him, although he made no attempt to flee.

Hooley marched up to him. “Get up please, Mr Webb. I’m arresting you on conspiracy to murder and conspiracy to pervert the course of justice.”

He decided that would do for now. By the time the investigation was complete, there would be many more offences to follow. It was just a pity that he couldn’t be charged with the destruction of his own family.

Mrs Webb had closed her eyes and didn’t open them again. Hooley imagined she must have been trying to block this development out.

To his surprise, Peter Webb looked relieved as the handcuffs went on. He looked at his wife. “It was only ever about money, to make us more comfortable,” he said. “I didn’t expect them to harm Edward.”

It was the final straw for his wife. Screaming incoherently, she rose from her chair and dug her nails into his face, cutting into the flesh around his eyes so that he was covered in blood. Then she sank back into the chair as two officers ran in.

"We need a doctor for Mrs Webb," He glanced at her husband. "Give him a tissue, for now, he can wait to see someone after we get him over to Victoria."

As Webb was led away, he started pleading with his wife. "You have to believe me. It was all for us. We'd have never had to worry about money again," His tone hit a whining pitch as she turned her back after giving him a look that was pure hatred.

Hooley got on the phone to his duty inspector. "I'm on my way – but we need to get a medic there. Mr Webb said something that his wife didn't agree with..."

"Given what he's done, I think he's lucky she didn't kill him." came the reply. "And, by the way, I've just got off the phone to Tom Phillips' crew. The operation is underway, and Mr Roper is part of it. The Major has asked for radio silence unless it's vital. I thought I'd check with you first."

56

Despite only wearing a thin suit, Roper was impervious to the cold. He was itching to go further, but Tom had been emphatic. "Until I know we have all the bad guys, I don't want you near there."

Fifty feet further down, the Major had just turned off his image intensifiers. The electric light spilling from the room ahead was dazzling after the darkness, and he and his men were forced to wait as their vision recovered.

Straining their eyes, they peered into the gloom. No-one spotted anything, so he gingerly started edging towards the light.

When he got a few feet away, he spotted Edward Webb sitting on a bed. There was someone else, but he couldn't make out who it was.

Beckoning two men closer, he told them he was going in first. The plan agreed, he got closer, then charged in. He was looking for a gang member and was relieved to see Gerald Stone instead.

"You're both safe now. Where are the others?"

Stone was so overwhelmed that all he could do was sob. The Major had seen this type of reaction before and knew it would be a while before he could help.

The teenager, on the other hand, was in good shape.

"They've got Daisy and Ricky. They took him ages ago, but she's only just gone again. She's been told that, if she doesn't kill Ricky, they will kill her."

"Do you know where they are?"

"I can show you the way. It's a sort of underground theatre. She said Ricky is tied to a post near the stage and they're going to make her line-up a crossbow and fire it."

Taking the boy into danger was out of the question, but he could get directions. Moments later, the Major, together with four of his men, approached a door that led, according to Edward, into the stage area.

Very gingerly, he opened the door. At first, there was nothing – but then he heard a gruff voice shouting, the words seeming to vibrate in the air as the sound echoed.

He couldn't see the space they were in, but judging by the echoes, it was a large space, at least double-height, and he sensed it was like a large hall, only underground. It smelt dusty and damp, and the cold was a physical sensation, sinking into bones.

The harsh voice boomed out again. "Do it, you silly little bitch!"

"I can't. I just can't!" Daisy's distress was evident. After forcing the words out, she began convulsing, her lung sucking in air as though she was at risk of drowning.

She was shown no pity. "Well, that makes you a daft little tart, doesn't it? I told you the rules. Kept it nice and simple so that even someone like you could follow them.

"But let me remind you about the biggest rule of all. If you don't do what you're told, there will be consequences. And the consequence is… you die. We'll still do him, of course."

The Major heard Daisy cry out; then, the man spoke again. "Any last words?"

Outside, the Major went for a count of three and dived in, his men right behind. The first thing he saw was a man holding a wicked-looking knife to Daisy's throat. The man didn't hesitate and made to cut her throat, actually starting to drag the blade as the first bullet went into his forehead, followed by a second. Instantly, the knife fell from his lifeless fingers. The Major heard more gunshots and turned to see two men falling to the ground, guns dropping out of their hands. He guessed the hooded figure, still standing, was Ricky.

By now, the second squad had turned up, and the Major's men were racing through the area. There was a shouted challenge he couldn't quite make out, then more gunfire, followed by a crash. Being forced to rely on his hearing made everything surreal.

It turned out the smashing sound was a large glass jug. Containing a clear liquid which a now lifeless gang member had been on the point of feeding to a bedraggled group of men and women. By the light of the torches, he could make out about fifteen people. He guessed the jug had contained poison which they were supposed to drink.

He heard more shouting from his men and some lights came on to reveal a glass-panelled room. People inside could be seen holding their hands in the air. It looked like Roper was going to be right about everything. More lights came on, and he realised he had been mostly correct about the space. It was an oblong about 100 feet deep, with the ceiling in shadow. At one end was a rudimentary stage with seating for the audience. The glass-fronted room was presumably the gallery area for controlling filming. He was still taking it all in when Roper ran in.

"Have you got the clown? He's the main one."

The SAS man cursed. He'd had no sight of him.

It was Daisy who surprised them all, her energy levels high with the exhilaration of escaping what must have felt like certain death. The dark circles around her eyes, and her ragged hair, contradicting the way she sounded.

"I've seen him go around the back of the stage. I think he must have a room there."

Roper was off. Sprinting like a champion, he raced off and ran from view. The Major, driven by instinct, was right behind him.

Roper's voice rang out. "He was hiding behind here... He's making a dash for it... I think he might be heading for the railway tunnels!"

The Major made his way to where he thought Roper was and was just in time to see him disappearing around the end of a long tunnel. Cursing, he ran after him and became aware he could hear the unmistakable sound of a moving tube train. Faced with this frightening new danger, he pushed harder but couldn't close the gap on Roper who was running as though his life depended on it.

Up ahead, Roper was oblivious to everything apart from the need of grabbing the clown. On and on he ran through the gloom. The clown was getting closer to the tunnels and the area he was in vibrated with the passing of a tube train. The clown raced around a corner with Roper just feet behind. The clown kept going, and it appeared he might be heading for the live tunnels. Roper found a burst of speed, and he was on top of the clown, pulling him down as they both smashed against the ground. Both men ignored the pain, and the clown started to drag himself forwards. Roper hadn't realised they were on a disused platform until another train shot through, illuminating the struggling pair in the flickering light from the carriages.

Meanwhile, the Major had caught up and had thrown himself towards the struggle. He arrived to find Roper hanging on to the Clown with everything he had. There was no way the man was getting away, despite his increasingly frenzied attempts to do so. He was beating Roper around the head and face... it had no effect. To help him realise his impossible predicament, the Major grabbed his hands in a grip that suggested it could crush bone.

With the tables turned all the fight went out of the clown.

"You're hurting me," he whined.

"Good," said the major, hauling him to his feet and handcuffing his hands behind his back. He ignored complaints they were too tight.

"Let's have a look at who's under there," he said, pulling off the mask.

There was total silence as his real face was revealed.

"Who are you?" asked Roper.

57

Tom Brady, the ideas man behind Smythe Smythson at Wakey Wakey, was the clown. A fact he had revealed after spending his first hour in custody refusing to talk. But then he announced he wanted to "to set the record straight"… and he would only do it by talking to Roper and Hooley.

This later part was no obstacle, and the three men found themselves in a large interview room at Victoria. A solicitor employed by Brady was also present. There was a table big enough to seat the four comfortably, and illumination came from an overhead strip light. A voice-activated recorder was on the table and cameras on the ceiling ensured a 360-degree view plus additional audio capacity.

The two detectives had tossed a coin as to who would ask the first question and Hooley had won. Now he took a sip of water as he looked at Brady. In costume, he had looked big and menacing, sitting in the interview room, he looked small and insignificant. The kind of man you wouldn't look twice at. He was small farmed and had thinning brown hair with watery blue eyes. His only notable feature was his mildly protruding ears.

Hooley wasn't in the mood to beat about the bush. "What made you come up with such a terrible scheme? Murdering people to provide thrills for your viewers."

Brady sighed, glanced at his solicitor, and leaned forwards, licking his lips before answering. "If you bear with me you will have all the answers you need… but let me tell this in my way."

Hooley shrugged and gestured with his hands. "So long as we get there, I don't mind the route we go down."

Brady leaned back, his eyes half-closed, and he briefly looked as though he had mentally drifted away. Then he began speaking in a clear, confident voice.

"I spent twenty years working as that man's producer and never once did I get the credit I deserved. He is a great talent, there is no doubt about that, the camera loves him, and he understands popular journalism, but it was my ideas that put him there.

"Three years ago, he won every prize going, Interview of the Year… I set that up and briefed him. It was that mother who lost three children to sudden death syndrome. And it was me coming up with the idea of turning school dinners vegan, to make healthier children and save the planet from CO2 emissions in producing meat… that won him Campaign of the Year. After that, he was a shoe-in for TV Personality of the Year.

"But tell me did you ever once hear him congratulate anyone, let alone me.? He was conscientious about thanking his team; like his make-up artist made the difference. Not that I expected anything, not after all this time. But do you know what tipped me over the edge?"

He glared fiercely at Hooley, who shook his head and said. "Please carry on."

Brady carried on. "He won an enormous pay rise and profit related bonus. It ran into millions of pounds. I thought he won't give me credit, but he can give me more pay. The greedy bastard only went and turned me down. He told me I should reflect on what an honour it was to work for him.

"I must admit that I went a bit crazy. I took a couple of weeks off and went on a bender for a few days. I woke up one morning and had the plan, right there."

He tapped his head, indicating his brain, and took a large swallow of water. Hooley copied him, but Roper sat quite still.

He carried on. "I decided to combine social media and television but do it a way that tapped into the worst of both. After all, whoever said creativity has to be highbrow? People out there…" he said, waving an arm at the world, "have no scruples. There's nothing they won't watch if they can get away without being caught. Well, that's what I offered. The chance to actually have someone killed. And have it done without any risk of being caught and all done on Prime Time."

He was looking feverish; his eyes were shining brightly, and his forehead was shiny with sweat.

"Would you like to take a break? Asked Hooley. "Can I get you anything?"

Brady shook his head. "No, nothing thank-you. I'm almost there. The best plans are always the simplest.

"People love the fact they can hide behind social media accounts and demand the most terrible things. But I knew that would be the case. You should see some of the emails we get at Wakey Wakey. You get the type of hypocrite who pretends to like a celebrity, then won't pay a penny to help them. Proves how much an Instagram account means anything. Then, there are the people out there with depraved minds who relish causing pain to others."

Hooley thought there was a depraved mind in the interview room but kept that thought to himself.

He said. "One thing that bothers me. Why did you make it a competition with Jonathan and me? It's not as if we could have added anything."

Brady leaned forward again. "You won't remember this, but you gave a big press conference a few years back, talking about online crime. I liked what you had to say, well, what Mr Roper had to say and built you into the plan.

"I started in Europe to get things rolling smoothly. Then it was over to London, where we have a vast media industry. I wanted to test myself, feel what it was like to be 'the top dog'. 'The number one'. You have to admit it, I had you both going for a while. But I got a bit overambitious in the end."

After his arrest, Peter Webb wouldn't stop talking. He claimed he was the victim, after stumbling across the money laundering operation out of his firm. He insisted Maria Morton had been placed as his PA to keep an eye on him.

He also insisted that he had only ever spoken to the clown on the phone. The man had told him that he just needed to get the London end of the money through and they would leave.

He also made the bizarre claim that the threats against his son were really threats against him.

"They were showing me what might happen if I didn't cooperate. Edward was never in any real danger."

His claims had infuriated Hooley, but he cheered up when he spoke to prosecutors who said they had enough on Webb to put him away for many years.

At MI5, Jenny Roberts had held out against a deal, so Hardy had remained as silent as the director. Verity Wade even refused to speak at the court hearings, so was quickly found guilty and sentenced to life without parole.

For Hardy – who, as an MI5 employee, had signed the Official Secrets Act – there was special treatment. Like Verity, she refused to take a plea, so a secret court session was quickly arranged. Her sentence and location are now a state secret.

The case had generated a lot of paperwork, which the self-proclaimed Odd Bods had ploughed through carefully. On the second Friday of the wrap-up, Hooley decided it was time for a celebration.

"How about drinking a few pints of lager and then eating so much curry we risk bursting?" he asked.

Roper was instantly against it.

"That's terrible. That type of binge drinking and eating is very bad for you. I am amazed you even thought it was a good idea."

"Jonathan," said Hooley. "Do shut up."

"Yeah, shut up, Roper," said Brooker. "I vote we get rat-arsed and then see who can eat the most poppadoms."

THE END

Thank you for reading my fifth book in the Jonathan Roper Investigates series.

I wanted to create a character who was a little bit different, and I think Roper fits that bill. His autism and lack of social skills provide him with both insights and problems. My sense that Roper would be an interesting fit for the modern world was influenced by my autistic son. He is non-verbal, but despite this, it has been heart-warming to see him develop; partly down to the brilliant support of so many carers, but also because of his own determination. This determination is a trait he shares with Roper. It was always my intention that the Roper series should be regarded as a series of "page-turning thrillers", each one capable of being read alone. While it offers some small insights into the autistic world, I also wanted to show some of the unexpected sides of autism. There can be humour there, and I hope that my portrayal of the relationship between Roper and his long-suffering boss, Brian Hooley, demonstrates that.

If you have read my other novels, you will know that I am a self-published author, and as I have mentioned writing a review on Amazon is really helpful as the number of reviews a book accumulates on a daily basis has a direct impact on sales. So just leaving a review, no matter how short, helps make it possible for me to continue to do what I love… writing.

Be the first to receive news on new Jonathan Roper and Brian Hooley adventures by visiting my website at **www.michael-leese.com** and become a VIP reader (I promise to only contact you with news of new launches). You can also write to me at the following email address: **hello@michael-leese.com** – I always enjoy reading your comments and thoughts about Roper, Hooley, Mayweather and the new “oddbod” team. - I do my best to respond to all correspondence.

Printed in Great Britain
by Amazon

42002604R00161